This one is for Kendra.

I0723488

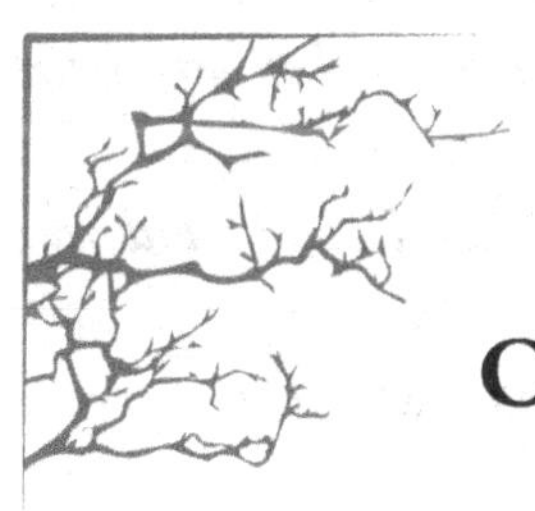

Chapter One

Toby

Mr Grandace's magic sent out a call. Julianna and Zo's power resisted at first, then it intertwined with his.

I stood in the school corridor, my classmates and former teachers joining me to make a half circle. In front of us were three doors, behind which Callie's dad and Miss Trager's siblings were being held prisoner.

Mr Grandace moved on to me and Asher, his magic reaching out for us like it would swallow us whole. I didn't want this. I didn't want to be joined to these people.

It wasn't the same as last time. Then, my magic had reached out, and my classmates' had reached back as if it had been something we were all subconsciously waiting for. This felt forced, unnatural.

Callie squeezed my hand, and I opened my eyes. Mr Grandace's magic reached out for her, ready to bind her to her father and Miss Trager's siblings.

I gave her a nod, trying to tell her it would be okay. But would it?

Callie jolted backwards, as if something invisible had slammed into her. She opened her mouth, but nothing came out.

"Callie!" I screamed. A second slam threw her across the room, ripping her hand from mine.

Toby! she screamed inside her head. And then all I could hear was static.

I ran towards her, but power threw me back. Then everyone was on the ground.

Tattered strings of magic hung in the air. I reached for my connection to Callie and found only shreds. The newly formed connections to Miss Trager and Mr Grandace were gone too. Our circle had been cut in half.

"Callie!" I called again. I tried to get up, but it was like moving through toffee.

A stab of pain shot through me, doubling me over. Not my pain – Julianna's pain echoing through Zo's mind. Zo's thoughts distorted, like a radio not quite tuned to a station. The thread between us was still there, but weakened, only just holding together.

"The circle is complete," Elijah said. It didn't sound like his voice. He turned, walking to the locked door and opening it. His movements were jerky, robotic. He unlocked the next door, then the third.

No one else moved. Everything seemed to be in slow motion, all of us suspended in a strange, liminal space. Miss Trager's sister walked out of one of the rooms, and then Callie's father appeared.

Callie stood, her movements just as jerky as Elijah's had been. She greeted her father with a hug. Her eyes darted around the room, panic filling them.

"I have to go," she said. The words seemed to terrify her.

Elijah took one of her hands, and her father took the other. They started to walk away.

"No!" Miss Trager yelled. "Ben, please don't do this!"

Mr Grandace threw out a spell. It fizzled in the air, disappearing.

I couldn't move. All I could do was watch as Miss Trager's siblings and Callie's father walked out of the school, taking Callie and Elijah with them.

"TOBY!" ZO HISSED.

I blinked, clearing my head of images from the night Ben had taken Callie and Elijah. No matter where I was, every moment of quiet had my mind slipping back there.

"I'm okay," I told Zo, though I was about ready to burst with anxiety.

We were crouched in the bushes at the edge of a parking lot. In front of us was a tower block office building. If Mr Grandace was right, then Callie and Elijah were inside.

The chill of the night turned my breath to steam. I covered my mouth with my collar, breathing into my sweatshirt. It was midnight-dark, likely no one would notice the tiny puff of crystalised air escaping from my lips, but I couldn't take the chance.

It had been three months since Ben had taken Callie and Elijah. Three months of him dragging them from place to place, never staying anywhere for more than a few nights. Three months of us trying to find them, knowing he was stealing their magic and forcing them to create destruction and chaos to further fuel his powers. We saw the aftermath of it all the time – burnt out buildings, withered wildlife, people injured or stripped of energy to the point of collapse. This was the first time Mr Grandace had managed to predict where they might strike – the first time we might actually have a shot at stopping it.

"Hey," Zo whispered. "Surveillance only, remember?"

I nodded, but if I got the chance to grab Callie, I would be taking it.

I froze as a low hum rose at the base of my skull, tickling the back of my mind.

"Callie?" I whispered. No answer came, but the humming continued. What was that sound? I'd heard it vibrating through my bones every time we got close for the last few months, but I still had no idea where it came from.

I peered into the darkness. Everything was still, too still. Then, more vibrations started, discordant notes competing against each other. I clapped my hands over my ears. Between the notes, I heard something else. The slithering of vines crawling towards me.

"Dammit!"

My classmates burst from their hiding places. Zo shrieked as a vine reached her. No... no! I just needed a moment longer. I'd heard Callie, I was sure of it!

"What are you doing, Toby? Get out of there!" Asher ran past me, Julianna just a step after him. Explosions boomed behind us, the flash of light blinding me for a moment. But still, I didn't move. I strained, listening for that first humming note, for Callie.

"Toby!" Zo grabbed my arm, yanking me up. She dragged me along behind her, half physically, half with magic. The bush where I'd been crouching exploded a second later. I turned back, but Zo's magical hold pulled me forward. Suddenly, I understood how Callie and Elijah must have felt, being on the ends of our magical human chain.

"Seriously, get it together!" Zo shook my arm. "We're losing them."

That got my attention. So much for surveillance. I turned, racing to keep up with her. We'd been close so many times, but we'd never quite managed to catch Callie or any of the others. She was here tonight, though, I was sure of it.

Ahead of us, Asher and Julianna ran towards the building entrance. I couldn't see Miss Trager or Mr Grandace but they would be here, somewhere. This watch and wait was their plan after all. They had traced Ben to this building, traced the signs of his destructive magic and chaos. We had to stop him – we had to get Callie and Elijah free of him.

A ball of fire flew from the front entrance, knocking Asher and Julianna to the ground. I grabbed Zo, flinging her down and covering her with my body as the flames rushed over us.

The fire turned green above us, morphing into a twisted tangle of vines and leaves. Julianna and Asher didn't move. I scrambled to my hands and knees, crawling over to them, keeping low.

Julianna groaned, eyes closed, but Asher raised his head. "Go! We're fine. They're getting away!"

Figures darted through the smoke and footsteps hit the pavement around us. I dragged myself up, stumbling after them. Zo scrambled to her feet too, giving chase.

We couldn't let them get away; it might be months before we got another chance. We'd seen their patterns, hiding for weeks, then reappearing to cause chaos as they drained whole city blocks of energy, taking it from everyone and everything to fuel their magic.

The smoke obscured my vision, but I kept running, desperate not to let them get away this time. Suddenly, I felt someone move. I reached out, clasping hold of their arm. My palm jolted, familiar bolts of electricity shooting off their skin. They spun around, hitting me, nails scraping across my face as they tried to free themself.

"Callie," I breathed.

She gasped. "Toby." Her voice cracked. She swayed like she was trying to take a step towards me, then a shuddering sound broke through her lips. "I'm sorry," she whispered.

"Please just come—" a blast of magic threw me back, wrenching her from my grip. She stumbled, falling to her knees. Lank hair fell over her face, haunted eyes staring out from behind it. The blast knocked the air out of me, but I tried to pull myself towards her.

She shrank back, like a wounded animal. She was all angles, sharp collarbones sticking out from the neck of her shirt.

"Please, Callie," I whispered. "Let me help you."

Something seemed to break inside her. She reached out a hand, but before I could grab it, her father was beside her. His arm snaked around her waist, and he pulled her to her feet. The discordant humming melody intensified, blocking out everything else inside my head. Callie met my eyes once more, and tears pooled in hers.

Joe dragged her away, and they were gone.

Footsteps pounded behind me. "Are you okay?" Zo asked. She grabbed my chin, turning my face to hers.

I jerked away. "I'm fine," I said, my voice rough. "But they're gone. I couldn't stop her."

Zo ran a few paces, as if she could catch up with them anyway, but she quickly gave up, returning to my side.

I leaned forward, hands on my knees as I tried to catch my breath. "I saw her, Zo. We were this close."

She nodded, and her lips pressed together into a thin line. I peered into the smoke and the remains of the disintegrating vines, desperate to catch one last glimpse of Callie. Was it too much to hope that she'd dropped some kind of clue? I prayed for a glass slipper or trail of breadcrumbs left in her wake.

Instead, another of Ben's victims stood in the wreckage. I stumbled forward. "Hey! You there, wait!"

The man turned towards me, and a violent vibrated note reverberated in my head. I took a few steps towards him, but then flames exploded around him.

"No! Oh god, no!" I lurched forward, but Zo grabbed me.

"Toby, you can't!"

"We can't leave him!"

"I know." She closed her eyes. Her magic swelled up around us. I poured my own into her, letting her use it. The flames let off swirls of energy. They flew up into the air, then began to coil, joining together into one long rope of power.

I grimaced. Ben was calling the energy back to him.

Is that man okay? Zo said inside her head. The flames died down, her power counteracting them. The man lay on the ground, shivering. No burn wounds marked his skin, but only because Zo had stopped the fire. I could feel from here that Ben had stolen a dangerous amount of energy from him. How many times had Ben made Callie or Elijah hurt someone like this? How many more people had Ben killed when we weren't here to stop him?

I turned away. "He's fine. Let's go find the others."

Zo stared at the man for a moment longer, biting her lip, then she linked her arm through mine. She leaned heavily against me, though she tried to disguise it. I couldn't say I was doing much better. I heard thoughts chasing themselves through her head, too fast to catch.

"I know it doesn't feel like it, but this is a good thing," she said aloud. "We found them. It means Mr Grandace's methods are working."

I frowned, not even dignifying that with an answer. Letting them get away wasn't "working". For that matter, I wasn't convinced Mr Grandace really had "methods". All he seemed to do was pore over the gibberish in Callie's mother's prophecy, and study news reports for signs of destruction that could be linked to Ben.

If I hadn't faffed about in that bush, maybe I would have been able to help Callie. I swallowed, ignoring the fact that she'd just blasted me with her magic. Was she like this all the time now? Did she have no control over her life or her actions? The thought made something compress around my chest as if I was the one trapped.

Zo stopped. Her arm slipped from mine as I kept walking.

I looked up, then my steps ground to a halt. "Oh my god!"

Asher lay face down in the dirt in front of us. Zo broke into a run, the soles of her shoes hitting the concrete hard. I stumbled after her, my feet clumsy underneath me.

Ben stood over Asher. Dark red magic swirled around Ben, stolen from Asher.

"Hey!" I yelled. "Get away from him." I raised my hands, willing my reactive magic to sprout into action. Zo did the same, racing towards him.

Ben flicked a wrist and Zo flew backwards, landing with a crash. He stepped towards her, and I launched myself forward, trying to get between them. He flung me back too. Murky red-black energy slipped from my skin, flowing out towards Ben. I clawed at it, trying to catch hold. It slipped through my fingers.

Ben shuddered as it reached him, his outline blurring almost as if the extra magic reshaped him. My head swum and the world closed in at the sides.

"No!" Julianna screamed.

Suddenly, she was beside Ben, launching herself at him. She shoved him, not with magic, just with sheer force. He stumbled back, startled. She raised her hands, landing a punch before he could right himself. She hit him again and again.

I blinked hard, trying to stay conscious. He was getting up. He was walking towards her.

"Jules!" I yelled. I tried to stand but my limbs felt leaden.

Ben raised his hands, and Julianna cowered. Asher's eyes opened. He scrambled up, throwing a magical blast at Ben.

Zo followed suit, a weaker attack exploding from her hands. I got to my feet, but my magic was spent. Instead, I grabbed Zo's arm, using our connection to give her the little energy I had left. Ben was strong, but surely he wasn't stronger than the four of us... except he was. He stood tall in the face of our attack, it barely seeming to register.

Julianna hit him again. She stomped on his foot, then kicked his shin. He backed away from her blows, breaking into a run.

None of us had the energy to chase. We watched him disappear into the smoke, almost as if he was turning into it.

"What the hell were you thinking?" Zo yelled at Julianna. "Did you really just *punch* him?"

Julianna had been funny about using magic since we got back to the school, but launching herself at Ben with nothing but high school self-defence skills was reckless beyond words. Yet somehow it had worked.

Julianna shook her head, then her legs gave way. Asher caught her, moving to do it almost before she started to fall. She buried her face in his chest, and her whole body shook, all the strength she'd displayed just moments before gone. Asher met my eye over the top of her head.

"How the hell did she just do that?" I asked.

Asher shook his head. "I have absolutely no idea."

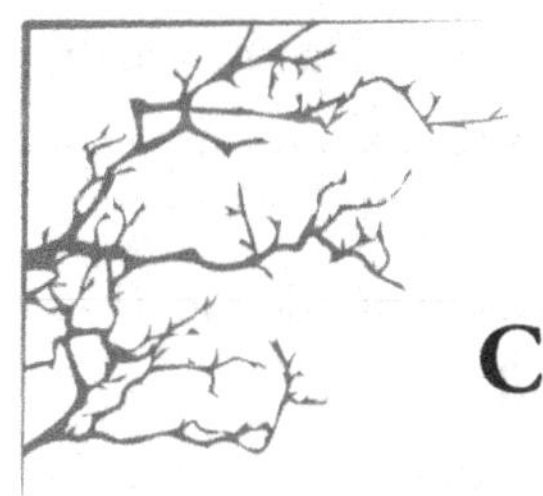

Chapter Two

Toby

We walked back to the meeting point in silence. The streets were empty – unnaturally so. We were in an industrial area on the outskirts of a suburb. The people living nearby would have no understanding of what happened tonight. They might have heard the explosions, they might have seen the flames, or even the plants growing out of control, but they would never put the cause down to magic. They would hunker down for the night in their nice safe homes, and in the morning, they would do everything they could to forget about it. I just wished we could do the same.

Asher supported Julianna, practically carrying her to keep her moving. I couldn't tell whether she'd been hurt again or if old wounds had opened up – physically and metaphorically. Either way, Asher's worry circled her, shutting me and Zo out.

Miss Trager and Mr Grandace hadn't joined us at the office building. They'd left us to keep watch but were supposed to return later in the night. I couldn't help feeling there was a reason they hadn't. What hadn't they told us about tonight? Somehow, they always managed to leave out the most important details.

Of course, there was another possibility – that they hadn't joined us because they'd been hurt or worse. I shook my head. I couldn't let myself think about that.

Zo bumped my shoulder, falling into step beside me. *What happened tonight?* she said inside her head.

"Huh?" I responded out loud, not willing to have her delve too far into my thoughts. Gravel and broken glass crunched under my feet, and I kept my eyes on it, kicking stray pieces along in front of me.

Zo clicked her tongue. "You were all over the place. I know you lose it every time you see Callie, but—"

"I didn't lose it." I thought of that bush exploding just after I got clear of it, and my confidence in my own words wavered. "I knew she was there. I could hear her."

Zo frowned. She didn't argue with me, but I heard it all in her thoughts. She didn't believe me about the humming. I wasn't connected to Callie anymore; Ben had severed my link to her and Asher's to Elijah, leaving only me, Zo, Julianna and Asher connected in our magical chain. I shouldn't have been able to hear anything from Callie, but somehow... somehow, there was that vibration every time I got close. Somehow, there was still electricity when I'd touched her skin.

Zo's eyes flicked away from mine, and my cheeks heated. "Sorry," I muttered. Thinking about Callie sometimes took us into uncomfortable territory. I schooled my mind back to safer topics.

Zo's steps slowed. I looked up, taking in the empty bus shelter ahead. Mr Grandace and Miss Trager had told us to meet them here if we got separated, but there was no sign of either of them.

"They're not here," Zo said, rather redundantly.

Asher cursed under his breath, and my stomach lurched. I glanced back the way we'd come, ready to turn back and start searching, but Zo strode ahead, picking something up off the bench.

"Looks like they left us a ride home." She held up a handful of silver bracelets.

Julianna let out a noise that was somewhere between a gasp and a groan. Honestly, I felt like doing the same. I'd never been a fan of our teacher's magical handcuff bracelets, but after learning they'd belonged to Callie's dead mother, they straight out creeped me out.

"At least it means they're alive," Zo said, responding to my unspoken thoughts.

Asher's jaw tightened. "That's a weak-ass silver lining."

Irritation flooded Zo's thoughts, but she turned away from Asher, a slight eyeroll the only visible sign of her mood. "Over here," she said. She pointed to a roughly drawn rune line on the ground beside the shelter.

As much as the woman frustrated me, I couldn't help but admire Miss Trager's quick thinking in setting this up. The rune line was shakily drawn, the symbols scratched out in pink chalk. A broken stick of it lay abandoned on the ground beside the last rune. I pocketed it just in case I ever needed to repeat the trick.

Zo doled out the bracelets. I slipped one on each wrist, but Julianna backed away.

"No... I can't. I can't do it."

Asher wrapped his arm around her. "It's okay. We can find another way home."

Zo scoffed. "Like what? Are you going to piggyback her ten kilometres?"

Asher frowned at Zo's flippancy, and he opened his mouth to snap back, but Zo turned to Julianna, placing her hands on her shoulders.

"I know you hate using magic, but it will be two seconds and then we'll be back safe at the school, okay?" Zo stared straight into Julianna's eyes, and I could almost believe she was using mind control.

"You don't have to," Asher said again. "If you want—"

"It's fine." Julianna took a long deep breath. "I just want to get out of here." She took two of the silver bands from Zo. Her hands shook, and it took her a moment to fit them to her wrists, but then she stood up straight, raising her head high.

Asher studied her face for a moment. I heard echoes of their silent conversation passed on through Zo's mind, and Zo and I both looked away. That part was harder for Zo than me.

Finally, Asher nodded. He put on his own bracelets, then wrapped his arm around Julianna's shoulders. Zo gave her a firm nod, which Julianna returned.

It amazed me how they did that – figured out what Julianna needed between them. Whether Asher and Zo liked it or not, the three of them were a team. I just wished seeing it didn't give me a lonely ache in my chest.

I slipped my hand into Zo's, squeezing it tightly. *Okay?* I said inside my head.

She nodded and squeezed my hand back. It didn't completely remove the lonely ache – only Callie would be able to do that – but it eased it just a little.

As one, we stepped over the rune line. Darkness crushed in on me from all sides, knocking the air from my lungs. I forced myself not to inhale, not to panic in the vacuum. Just a moment longer and... light and sounds slammed back into me. I let go of Zo's hand, falling forward onto my knees.

"I will never get used to that," Zo said, as she landed with a thump on her butt.

Asher and Julianna arrived a bit further down the corridor. Asher pulled himself up immediately, moving to crouch in front of Julianna. He held her shoulders as she shook.

I couldn't imagine what it was like for her, reliving the moment she'd almost died every time we made one of these leaps. Even so, I wished we could teleport everywhere. It would make searching for Callie so much simpler, but the bracelets only worked to bring us back to the school, their magic tied to it. Occasionally, Callie's reactive magic had given her the ability to jump elsewhere, but that was the problem with reactive magic – you couldn't control it. It reacted to the moment, doing what it thought was right, whether or not you agreed.

Zo watched Asher and Julianna for a moment, then tore her eyes away. I did the same, giving Julianna the only small measure of privacy we could offer.

Zo pushed herself up and brushed imaginary dust off her shirt. "What are the chances they'll let us head to bed and sleep for a couple of hours?"

"Approximately zero to zero, give or take a margin of error." Even if they did let us sleep, I knew I wouldn't be able to. What the hell had happened that they just left us tonight?

As if in response to that thought, I felt a ping in my stomach. Zo rolled her eyes, something that was not quite a grin crossing her face. "Not even time for a bathroom break? Rude." She made her way down the corridor to the toilets anyway.

I considered refusing to go downstairs, making them come up to us. I wanted to see for myself that Miss Trager and Mr Grandace were safe, but I did not want to rehash the night. It wasn't like our teachers' "debriefing" meetings ever amounted to much. Ninety percent of the time, we wasted hours rereading cryptic paragraphs in Callie's mother's prophecy, trying to match them up to things that had already happened. I couldn't help with that. While the others all had moments where Sammy's writing revealed itself to them, I'd never been able to read so much as a word. It all looked like gibberish to me.

The magical ping pulled at my stomach again, more insistent this time. I sighed and ducked into my room, grabbing a hoodie. I pulled it on and wandered back into the hallway.

Asher emerged from Julianna's room, closing the door softly behind him. He stayed holding the doorhandle for a moment, his eyes closed, swaying ever so slightly. Then he looked up, meeting my eye. His jaw tightened.

"She okay?" I asked. *Stupid question, Toby. Of course she isn't.*

"She's just tired."

Somehow, I didn't think it was the type of exhaustion sleep would fix.

Asher made his way downstairs, but I hung back, waiting for Zo. She reappeared and linked her arm through mine.

"This place could really use a lift, huh?" She gave me a tired smile.

I shrugged. "I don't know. I kind of like the rhythm of the steps." I thumped down them as if to prove my point, letting gravity do half the work.

"Each to their own, I guess... weirdo." Zo bumped my shoulder. She let go of my arm and jumped the last two steps, landing on the other side of the rune line at the bottom. I felt the buzz as she crossed it, and she let off a couple of sparks. They died out too quickly to see the colour.

I frowned. When had I last seen red and gold sparks from Zo? In fact, when had I seen any magistations? Surely there'd been something tonight – some flash of fear or frustration? I couldn't remember. Perhaps we were all too numb to feel anything.

I stepped over the rune line myself, shuddering a little at the buzz.

We made our way down to the "planning room" on the second floor. Mr Grandace insisted on calling it that, but in reality, it was just one of the old classrooms. I think he was trying to show us he saw us as equals – that we were no longer his students, but something closer to colleagues in the fight against out-of-control magic. A better way to show us that would have been to stop ordering us around and actually tell us what was going on.

Zo hesitated outside the door, glancing back at me. Asher stood just inside the doorway, not fully entering the room either.

"What is it?" I asked.

Zo tilted her head towards the room, and I stared in. Mr Grandace strode across the floor, yanking several books off one of the shelves as he went. He flipped through them, scanning the covers, before grabbing another handful. Miss Caraway rummaged in a desk drawer, pulling out pens.

"I'm telling you; I left it on the table. It's gone," Miss Trager snapped as she scrawled something across the whiteboard, her pen squeaking in protest at how hard she was pressing. "They tripped the wards. One of them was in here."

Ben or one of the others was here? No wonder Miss Caraway and Mr Grandace had left us to fend for ourselves at the office building.

"They can't have taken it," Mr Grandace said.

"Well, it's gone! Stop tearing things apart and help me record what we can."

Mr Grandace hesitated, pinching the bridge of his nose with one hand. "Blast it. Okay." He dropped the books he was holding and whipped around to the whiteboard. Miss Caraway placed a whiteboard marker in his hand, and he joined Miss Trager in scribbling across the surface of the board.

Zo and I shuffled into the room. "What's going on?" I asked.

"The prophecy's gone," Miss Trager said, without looking up. "I'm sorry we had to leave you tonight, but the magic flung Arthur back here when someone broke in and tripped the wards. I only just had time to draw the runes before following."

Her words tumbled over each other, as if she was still rushing against the pull of the magic. This was too much information to take in all at once.

"The prophecy's gone?" I repeated, focusing on the only bit I understood. "Gone where?"

"Taken." Miss Caraway chucked a couple of pens in our direction. Asher caught one of them; the other landed at Zo's feet. "Write down everything you remember – everything you ever read." She clicked her fingers and pointed at the other white board.

Zo and Asher glanced at each other, then Zo picked up the fallen pen. They each took half of the whiteboard, beginning to write. I hovered, unsure what to do with myself. I had a vague memory of Callie reading something aloud when she'd first seen the book, but that wasn't going to be much use now.

"Was it him?" I asked.

Miss Trager didn't turn around. "Who else would want it?"

I shivered. Ben's looming figure was burned into my mind like the boogieman of childhood nightmares. I didn't know why the idea of him having the prophecy made that image so much more frightening. It wasn't like it had done us any good – most of the time the writing in it stayed stubbornly gibberish, and when it did unscramble itself into words, they were so cryptic we could only understand them after the fact.

"This is bad, right?" Zo asked. "Can he use the magic from it?"

None of the adults answered, but the lines around Miss Trager's mouth tightened. Mr Grandace just kept writing.

I hadn't thought about that part. Whatever magic Sammy had poured into the book must be incredibly strong. The idea of Ben gaining that, on top of the power he was siphoning from Callie, Elijah and everything else... well, it didn't bear thinking about. There was a reason Sammy and Miss Trager had fought so hard to keep their magic from him.

Asher gave up writing. "That's it. That's everything I remember."

Zo scrawled another couple of lines, then stopped too, her list of prophecy fragments running out. It wasn't surprising. Our former teachers had been protective of the book, only allowing us glimpses.

I scanned the lines Mr Grandace had written. He'd moved onto paper now, the board full. Unfamiliar strings of letters and words filled it, his writing devolving into nonsense.

"What are you...?" I trailed off. He was recording the gibberish. He'd run out of revealed prophecy and was now wasting time scrawling down the lines of unrelated letters Sammy had filled the pages with in her magical fugue state.

A part of me was impressed he could remember it... but a bigger part of me was suddenly really angry.

"This is bullshit!" The words exploded out of me.

Zo jumped, letting off a shower of sparks, and thunder crackled above us. So much for her being too numb to feel anything.

"Why are we wasting time on this?" I yelled. "Ben's escalating things, right? We need to get Callie out of there now!"

A small voice in the back of my mind told me I should be saying "Callie and Elijah," but a bigger voice knew that if it came down to it, I would leave him behind to save Callie, no question. I didn't want to think about what type of person that made me.

"Nothing has changed, Toby," Miss Caraway said. "It's still safer to leave Callie and Elijah where they are until—"

"What do you mean nothing's changed? He's getting more powerful and we're just watching him!"

Ben drew energy from everything around him, and magic where he could get it. The more chaotic the energy the better.

Those explosions today would be enough to fuel his magic for months, let alone adding Sammy's notebook into the mix.

"I know it's hard," Miss Trager's voice was flat, exhausted. "But I genuinely don't think Ben plans to hurt Calliope."

"What would you know? You didn't even notice he'd enslaved your own sister!"

"That's enough!" Mr Grandace stepped between me and Miss Trager. A coloured cloud of magic seeped out around him, forcing me to calm down. I didn't need it. Miss Trager's face had frozen at my words, and I instantly regretted them.

"I'm sorry," I said and meant it. "It's just... you didn't see Callie tonight. She looked..." I couldn't even bring myself to say it. She looked scared and in pain. She looked like she was dying.

Zo touched my arm, squeezing it, but I didn't get much comfort from the gesture.

Miss Trager blinked, seeming to properly take us in for the first time tonight. "You saw her?" Her face paled and she sank back against one of the chairs. "Oh god, it was just supposed to be surveillance! I never would have left you if I'd—"

"We're fine," I said sharply, cutting her off. I didn't know if that was true in Julianna's case, but it had to be. "We'll be okay. But Callie won't."

Miss Trager swallowed. "We will get them out of there as soon as we can, I promise."

Her voice came out tight. She meant that, I'm sure, but given she hadn't managed to free her sister or Callie's father in the sixteen years they'd been Ben's prisoners, I didn't have high hopes of "as soon as we can" being any time soon.

"It's been a long day," Miss Caraway said. "How about you all get some rest and you take us through everything in the morning?"

I wanted to argue, but Asher was already moving to the door, ready to head back upstairs to check on Julianna.

Zo took my arm, squeezing it tight. "Come on," she said. "Let's go get something to eat."

I opened my mouth to protest, but my stomach rumbled at the thought of food. I closed my eyes for a moment, trying to will the sensation away, but I wasn't stronger than my own biological needs. "Jules nearly defeated him tonight, you know?" I said.

"Toby…" Asher's voice was a warning, but I ignored it.

"What do you mean?" Miss Trager asked. I didn't think it was possible, but she turned a shade paler at the thought.

"She hit him. The magic did next to nothing, but she punched him and it nearly knocked him out."

The teachers looked at each other, a silent conversation passing between them. Then Miss Caraway stepped towards me. "Come on. You can tell me everything while we eat."

Asher and Zo both glared at me, on the same page for once. Was I doing the wrong thing by revealing what Julianna had done? She was so fragile these days. It might actually break her if our teachers interrogated her over what happened. Honestly though, I didn't care. I'd let them break all of us if it meant getting Callie back.

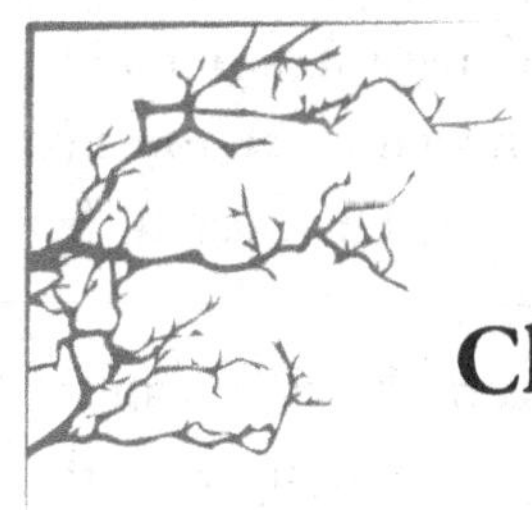

Chapter Three

Callie

Heavy sobs wracked their way through me. The sound echoed in the tiny room, the concrete walls and floor closing in on me. I pressed my face into my pillow, trying to stifle my tears. I'd seen him. I'd been close enough to touch Toby, and instead, I'd shoved him away. Not just shoved him, I'd sent a blast of magic throwing him backwards. Was he hurt? Did I even have the right to ask that?

A soft knock sounded against my door. I froze, pressing a hand to my lips to muffle my ragged breath.

Be silent.

Be still.

I wouldn't survive this if I couldn't make myself small.

"It's me," Elijah whispered. He opened the door just a crack, then slipped through closing it behind him. "You have to stop crying."

I nodded but even as I did, a muffled hicuppy sound came out of my mouth and my chest shook. Elijah clicked his tongue, irritated, then padded the two steps across the dark room to reach the edge of my mattress. I shifted over so he could join me.

He lay down next to me, then slipped his arms around me, pulling me against his chest. My skin tingled as he touched me, and suddenly I realised how cold I was. His warmth felt charged, and I moved closer.

He made a noise in his throat, shaking his head. "Of all the people I could have got stuck with, I had to end up with the one that cries all the time."

I let out a laugh, and he shushed me. I swallowed, the humour dying in my throat. We both froze, listening.

I had survived years in foster care by making myself small enough not to be noticed. Why was I finding it so hard to do it again now?

Elijah traced soft circles on my back, gently soothing me despite his purported annoyance with my tears. "You saw him tonight, didn't you?" He didn't say Toby's name, but it was obvious who he meant.

I frowned. "Yeah. Didn't you?"

"I can't see anything when Ben's controlling us."

I wasn't sure whether that was a good or a bad thing. We'd caused so much destruction over the past few months. I wished I could forget some of the things I'd seen, but a part of me wanted to bear witness to it. A part of me wanted to know exactly what awful things I was doing, even if I couldn't stop them.

"Toby grabbed me," I told Elijah. "I... I hit him."

I couldn't get Toby's face out of my head. The shock in his eyes when I threw him backwards, then the way they'd shifted as he stared at me. What did I look like to him? I knew my body had changed in the last few months – I knew *I* had changed, my brittle shell thickening, petrifying the few parts inside of me I'd managed to keep soft. How much of that showed on the outside?

Elijah pulled back a little to look at me. His eyes flicked back and forth between mine. "Toby will be okay," he said. "He's a weedy little loser, but he's tough as anything."

I raised my eyebrows. "You, giving Toby a compliment? My crying must really be annoying you."

Elijah shrugged. "You already know you're annoying, Cal. Don't make me say it."

I let out a silent half-laugh, and a smile tweaked the corners of Elijah's lips. I could feel his breath on my neck and suddenly this all felt way too intimate. I pulled back, angling my face away so I didn't have to meet his eye. Even so, I could feel him watching me. He didn't remove his arms from around me.

Even after all this time, it still felt strange to be this close to him. There was no magnetic charge forcing me away, no magic trying to tear us apart. His warm arms circling around me were one of the only safe places I had... but still, it felt wrong.

He seemed to sense some of what I was thinking, and his face closed off. He shifted away a little, not meeting my eye. I had to fight the urge to draw him back – to pull him closer.

"Now you're done leaking everywhere, can we give this a go before the others wake up?"

I let out a slow breath. Of course. He hadn't come in here to comfort me – he wanted to keep trying with his pointless attempts to fix our magic. I was annoyed to find a part of me was disappointed. I squashed that down and pulled myself up into a sitting position.

"Yeah, okay." My voice came out hollow – my lack of enthusiasm flattening it out.

He sat up and raised his palms in front of him, ignoring my lacklustre attitude. I half-heartedly raised mine, mirroring him.

He frowned, and grabbed my left hand, stretching my fingers out. "Can you concentrate, please?"

"Sorry." I tensed my fingers, putting more effort into keeping them flat. It was so strange how we had reversed roles. Elijah had always been the one the rest of us had had to reign in.

He closed his eyes, and I did the same, doing my best to "connect" to my magic. I felt it heavy and alien inside me, uncomfortable even after all this time using it. Honestly, I still found it hard to believe I had magic at all.

Elijah's energy reached out, finding the ends of the frayed connection between us. The loop of Ben's magic around me tightened as he did, almost as if Ben sensed our rebellion from the depths of his sleep. Elijah and I both froze, waiting. After a minute the constriction eased.

Elijah let out a breath. "It's okay. He doesn't know what we're doing."

Neither do we, I nearly said, but I kept the thought to myself. A few months ago, I couldn't have done that. Toby being able to read my thoughts had made me feel trapped at the time, but I'd had no idea how free I had really been. The bonds Ben held us with didn't join us in the same way that the connections to my classmates had. The rope of magic was only there for Ben's purposes – to contain us, to drain our energy, and when he deemed necessary, to puppet us like the slaves he believed we were.

Suddenly, magic flared in front of me. Tiny lines of fireflies lit up in the air, marking out the ends of my broken connection to Elijah. I gasped, pulling away, but they reached for me, stretching out to touch my fingertip.

"You can see it?" Elijah asked.

"Yeah."

"Take hold of the magic," he told me. "You can do it. It's yours."

It didn't feel like mine. I pinched the air next to one of the fireflies, gently tugging it towards me. It followed with little resistance.

Elijah let out a breath that was almost a laugh. "I *felt* that," he said.

"So, what do I do now?"

Elijah shrugged. "Let it tell you what to do. The magic should want to heal itself."

I frowned, but a second string of fireflies appeared, stretching out from my fingertips... almost as if they were reaching for Elijah, wanting to heal the bond between us just as he said.

The magic tickled against my fingertips, like insects crawling over my skin. They seemed to claw at me, just as disquieted by this as I was. My heart raced, and the fireflies jostled with each beat.

"Tie the ends together if you have to." A hint of impatience crept into Elijah's voice. "Just try something."

The pounding in my chest shot up a notch, and the fireflies blurred, their lines becoming less defined. I took a breath. New sparks lit up between me and Elijah, the fireflies guiding me like they always had.

I took hold of two tiny threads, one from Elijah, one from me. But as I did, other lines of lights lit up in the air, different colours fighting for my attention. I blinked, trying to focus on the remains of our connection. My eyes blurred, the pounding of my heart and the colours all too much.

Something slammed into me, throwing me back. I crumpled against the wall. Tiny flames burst into life on my skin, pain erupting with them. I drew breath to scream.

Suddenly, Elijah was beside me again, clapping his hand over my mouth. "Don't! Ben will hear you," he whispered.

The flames lapped at his palm, but he didn't let go. His fingers tightened against my cheek, flexing in pain.

God, it hurt. Nausea rolled through me, but the flames slowly shimmered then burnt out. *What was that?* I wanted to ask... but I already knew the answer.

Elijah removed his hand carefully. There was no sign of burn wounds. "I guess I still repel you," he said. His voice was tight, and it seemed to hold a question he didn't ask.

"I guess so." Something heavy settled in my chest.

We both fell silent. It wasn't like before. I wasn't being forced away from him – I could stay beside him without it hurting – but still... something in the magic didn't want the connection between us to be rebuilt.

His breaths were heavy, and I found myself matching my inhales to his.

"E?" I whispered.

He raised his head, but still didn't quite look at me. I slid my hand across the mattress, reaching for his.

The door opened. Elijah shot out of the bed. I froze, my throat tightening. A dark figure appeared, silhouetted in the doorway.

"Joe," Elijah said.

I let out a slow breath, mirroring Elijah's. Not Ben – just Joe.

Joe looked from me to Elijah, and my cheeks heated up. "I was crying," I blurted out. "Elijah—"

"Came to comfort you?" A scoff burst through Joe's lips, and there was no mistaking the sarcasm in his voice.

The heat in my cheeks turned to flames. "It wasn't like that," I mumbled. I couldn't blame Joe for his scepticism. Elijah had never been known for his empathetic abilities, and I knew what this must look like.

Elijah shrugged. "She was keeping me awake." He started towards the doorway, but Joe grabbed his arm.

"You need to watch yourself." Joe turned to me. "You both do."

I forced myself to look up – to hold Joe's eye. "Are you going to tell?" In another lifetime, we might have had this argument if I been caught sneaking out or hiding a boyfriend in my room, but there was no fatherly warmth or concern in Joe's face. All that flickered through his features was fear.

"I can't protect you if he catches you," he said.

"Well, it's a good thing he didn't." Elijah's voice dropped low, a hint of a threat in it.

Joe stared at him for a long moment and then he stepped aside, allowing Elijah space to leave the room.

Instead, Elijah glanced back at me. "We'll talk later, yeah?"

I made myself nod. I desperately wanted to flick my gaze to Joe, to see what he thought of this exchange. I didn't let myself. He was my father, yes, but I had no idea if he was on my side.

"Get to bed," Joe said. "Both of you."

I reluctantly settled back down on the mattress, though sleep was out of the question. Elijah gave a single nod of his head then turned away, leaving me with Joe.

Joe stared at me for a moment. He shook his head slowly, and I didn't know how to interpret the gesture.

"You need to be careful of him," he said finally.

"You got Mum pregnant at 17. You don't get to warn me about boys."

Joe blinked, and his mouth fell open, but no words came out. I shouldn't have said that. It was petty and cruel, but something about being around Joe turned me into a child.

"You don't need to worry," I said, my voice barely more than a mumble. "It's not like that with Elijah. He really was just trying to comfort me."

Comfort me and connect to my magic so we could escape, but Joe didn't need to know about that part.

"That's not what I'm worried about."

I glanced up, frowning. Joe looked like he wanted to say something more but instead he moved to the door.

"Just be careful, okay? I meant what I said – I can't protect either of you from Ben."

"You dragged me away from Toby tonight," I said. "Your lack of ability to protect me is pretty obvious. Don't try to act like a dad now."

Joe frowned, and I grimaced. I shouldn't have said that either. I wasn't supposed to be aware of anything that was happening while I was under Ben's control.

I studied Joe's face. Had he figured out what Elijah and I had been doing? Did he know that I wasn't under Ben's control in quite the same way he, Chloe and Elijah were? He didn't give anything away, just stared at me, his frown deepening until it seemed his face would crack.

"I'll be careful," I said, breaking the silence. "I promise."

His expression remained blank, no sign of whether that answer satisfied him or not, but he nodded and turned away. He closed the door behind him, blocking out the dim light from the corridor.

I lay back against the mattress. Even if Joe did know what we'd been planning, did it matter? For months, Elijah and I had been trying to regain the connection between us. I never thought we would manage to do it, but now I was realising it might not matter even if we did. We still repelled each other – polar opposites in the dangerous magnetic energy field we'd created.

I stretched my fingers out, feeling an echo of Elijah's magic pushing me back. I plucked at the thin threads of my own power, slowly coaxing the fireflies out. Why was this so different to my connection to Toby?

My heart squeezed at the thought of him. Toby had been right in front of me tonight. He had been within arm's reach, and I'd pushed him away. I let my eyes close, silently begging the universe for something else to fill my head.

Footsteps pacing the corridor answered. My eyes shot open. I clenched my fists, the fabric of the mattress gripped tightly in my hands as if that could somehow protect me. The footsteps got closer, until Ben was right outside my door.

Leave me alone, Ben, I whispered inside my head. *Please just leave me alone.*

He took a slow steady stream of energy from me at all times, but if he was coming closer, it meant he was going to take more. He kept the four of us prisoner, so he could get close enough to tear power from us, leaving us with next to nothing.

The loop of magic tying me to him tightened. It crushed my chest, forcing the air out of my lungs. But I could hear him breathing, right outside the doorway. Then I felt it, the slow drain speeding up, pulling more energy from me, taking away what little magic I had left.

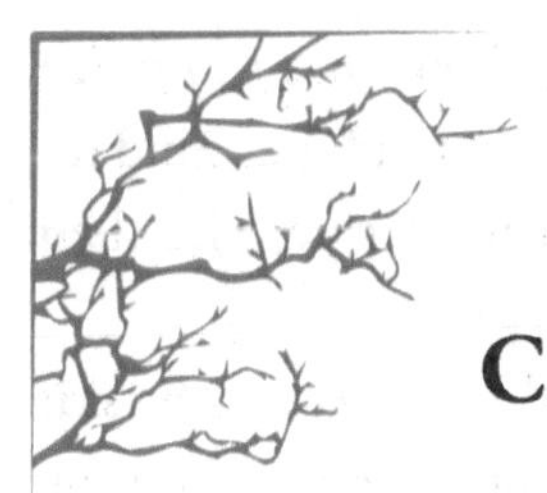

Chapter Four

Callie

In the morning, I lay on my mattress for a long time, hoping to fall back asleep. When I didn't, I tried teasing out the threads of magic again. The lines of fireflies swayed towards my fingertips every time I moved as if they were trying to help, but they still felt alien to me, like pressing against a limb numb with pins and needles.

Joe, Elijah and Chloe's voices floated through from the other room. I couldn't hear the words, but from the cadence, they were chatting about nothing. Sometimes these were the worst parts – when things were calm, almost normal. Almost normal, but also so far from it it hurt.

My door was ajar, and Mosby padded his way in.

"Hey, buddy." I reached out a hand, but Mosby went straight for my face, wet nose snuffling against mine.

"I don't have any food, bud."

Mosby licked my face to check anyway, then padded back out of the room. From down the corridor, I heard Joe greet him in a high-pitched, excited tone, then the answering thump of Mosby's tail.

Chloe had told me Joe found him stray a few years ago. A part of me wondered if Joe had been trying to replace me by keeping him, but I didn't like thinking about that too much. Whatever Joe's reasons, having a friendly Labrador around did make things less bleak. Perhaps that's why Ben had let them keep him.

I pulled myself upright, and my head swam. My skin burned, every touch of my clothes stinging. I stretched out my fingers, watching them shake. Ben must have siphoned even more energy than usual.

I dragged myself down the corridor to the bathroom. We'd stayed here a few times before – one of several places Ben had set up for us to squat. He shifted us every time his paranoia got to him, so I had no idea how long we'd be here before he felt the need to uproot us once again. I didn't understand how Chloe and Joe had survived like this for seventeen years.

This was an old factory. The bathrooms were rows of stalls and sinks, with only one cold and mouldy shower, but at least the toilets still flushed. We'd stayed in much worse places over the last few months.

I stared down at the plug hole. A tiny vine had crept up through the pipes overnight, spreading into the basin. Was it my magic or Joe's that had coaxed it to grow? I stared at the leaves, willing them to grow faster. An out-of-control plant like Toby's would surely disrupt Ben's magic enough to free us. Instead, the vine withered, curling up and retreating back down the pipes. I turned on the tap, flushing it away.

I washed quickly with cold water, standing over the sink, too nervous to fully undress. Sometimes Elijah and I stood guard for each other, but I still didn't trust Ben not to drag us away from here half-naked.

My hair clumped together in greasy strings, but there wasn't much I could do about that. Hopefully the next place he towed us off to would have hot water, or at the very least shampoo.

I made my way down to the old employee staffroom. It had cooking facilities, and the smell of something savoury made my stomach rumble. The power was off, of course, but Ben allowed Chloe and Joe enough use of their magic to deal with practicalities like that. If I asked nicely, she might even heat enough water for me to fashion a bath.

Joe and Elijah fell quiet as I came into the room. That bugged me – that Elijah was forming a relationship with my... Joe. It didn't feel right to call him my dad. I wasn't sure what he was to me, but it wasn't that.

Chloe handed me a plate of eggs. They were overcooked, and heavily peppered by the smell, but I took them gratefully. Chloe served up a plate for herself and sat down next to me.

When I'd first seen her, however many weeks ago it was, I'd thought she was Miss Trager. Now, I wasn't sure how I'd made that mistake. Sure, she had the same fair hair, but Chloe's face was harder, her manner flintier. Miss Trager had seemed broken the last time I'd seen her.

I shook my head, trying to clear the image, and shovelled a couple of forkfuls of eggs into my mouth. Almost immediately, my stomach objected. I forced myself to swallow but pushed the plate away.

"Too burnt?" Chloe asked.

I shook my head. "No, they're fine. My stomach just hurts."

Joe frowned. "You need to eat."

I looked up, meeting his eye, then shook my head. I was sure I'd vomit if I opened my mouth again. Chloe and Joe glanced at each other, then Chloe reached a hand across the table. Magic seeped off her, and I jerked away.

"Let me help you." Chloe's voice was low. "Joe's right, you have to eat."

I glanced between the two of them. Their expressions told me nothing. What had prompted this show of paternal concern?

Elijah gave a mocking shake of his head. "Only you could need magical help to eat a plate of eggs, Cal." His tone was light, but the muscles in his neck were tight, and I could feel his leg jiggling under the table.

Chloe gave me something which almost passed for a concerned smile. I must have looked worse than I thought if they were all this worried. Or perhaps they just wanted me to get stronger, so Ben didn't decide I was too weak and start farming more energy from them instead.

I picked up my fork, scooping another mouthful of egg on to it. Waves of magic flowed out from Chloe, competing with the waves of nausea. I resisted the urge to pull away this time. Despite myself, I relaxed into her power. My stomach eased, and I managed to eat another few bites before the sick feeling returned.

Chloe let the magic fall away. "Good. It's annoying when you let my cooking go to waste." She picked up my half-finished plate and took it out to the kitchen. Joe gave me a nod, then followed after her.

"What was that about?" I asked Elijah, once they were out of earshot.

"Huh?"

"The three of you staging a breakfast-intervention?"

Elijah rolled his eyes. "If you would just eat like a normal person—"

I touched his arm, making him stop. "E, what's going on?"

Elijah glanced towards the kitchenette, where Joe and Chloe stood together, speaking in low voices. Elijah let out a heavy breath, then nodded towards the door. "Outside."

I followed him down the corridor towards the dirt yard outside the factory. If you could call it a yard. The narrow strip of bare earth was a bleak parody, but I'd take any outdoor time over being trapped inside twenty-four seven. We stepped through the door, and immediately, the ropes of magic around me tightened, straining at the slight distance from the building. I stopped, breathing lightly as they constricted around my chest. *It's okay,* I whispered inside my head. *We're not trying to run.*

Slowly, the tension eased, allowing me the tiniest bit more freedom. We walked to the fence, leaning back against it.

"Would you believe it's just Joe trying to be a good dad and look out for you?"

I frowned. "No. And don't be an ass."

Elijah smirked. "Fine, no playing on your daddy issues."

"E..." A little pang of guilt hit under my ribs. Him bringing up my relationship with Joe was manipulative, but so was me using that nickname. I could tell he liked that I had a special name for him. I could tell he thought it meant more than it did.

He fiddled with a loose loop of wire on the fence. "Last night – it was a distraction. He was trying to draw Mr Grandace and the others out."

Draw them out for what? Something caught in my throat. "He didn't hurt them, did he?"

Elijah shook his head. "No, but he sent Chloe to the school."

"Why?" Was it bad that I hadn't noticed Chloe wasn't with us last night? In all the chaos, it had been hard to keep track of the others.

"He got her to take the prophecy."

I blinked. "You mean…"

"Your mum's prophecy, yeah. The one Miss Trager used to start all this bullshit."

There was a lot to unpack there. I'd held Mum's notebook for approximately two minutes before everything went to shit. Even thinking about it gave me *Feelings* with a capital F, but what did Ben want with it? He wouldn't be able to read it. Even if he could, all it ever seemed to have done was lead Miss Trager and Mr Grandace down dangerous and confusing paths, creating more and more chaos as they went.

"What does that have to do with me eating Chloe's gross eggs?" That was not the most important question by far, but it was the only one that felt safe to ask.

Elijah yanked the piece of wire, ripping it free from the fence. He stared at it, as if surprised by his own strength, and then tossed it across the yard, letting it land in the dirt. "He drained energy from you again last night, didn't he?" he asked. "After I left?"

I swallowed, fighting the urge to shudder. The hollow sound of Ben's footsteps walking towards my room echoed in my mind, as did the tight feeling of his magic constricting around my chest.

Elijah touched my arm, squeezing it gently. I couldn't help but notice that his hand closed nearly all the way around my bicep. Perhaps Joe and Chloe were right when they said I needed to eat.

"This could get worse," he said. "We need you to be strong. *I* need you to be strong."

I understood that, but a plate of burnt eggs wasn't going to steel me enough to break us out.

"Tonight, we'll try again, yeah?" he said. "With the magic?"

Dread built in my stomach at the thought of trying to persuade my magic to behave the way we wanted it to. "You really think that will work?"

Elijah studied my face for a moment, then slowly let go of me. His palm brushed softly down the length of my arm. There was no charge forcing me away this time. My skin tingled under his touch, and I had to resist the urge to shiver, but the contact didn't repel me, quite the opposite.

He said something under his breath. I wasn't sure I'd heard correctly, but it sounded like: "It might if you let it."

I automatically took half a step away but forced myself to stop there. Maybe he was right. Maybe last night was a fluke, and our magic wouldn't magnetically force us from each other if we tried again. Maybe...

"One more shot," I told him. "But after that, we stop. I can't keep getting my hopes up."

He nodded, relaxing a little now he'd got me to agree.

None of this really mattered anyway. Whether or not we managed to reconnect our magic, there was something much more important at stake now – the prophecy. We had to figure out a way to stop Ben using it. Nothing good ever came from that book, and I had a feeling we were all going to be sorry that Ben had got his hands on it.

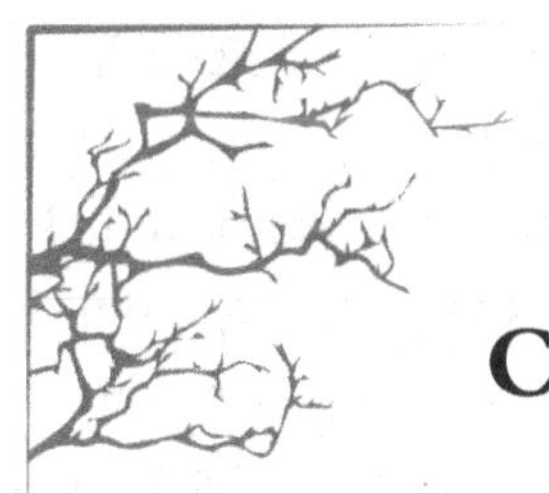

Chapter Five

Toby

I didn't sleep that night. Every time I closed my eyes, it was either Callie's face staring at me from behind my eyelids, or an echo of that humming. What was that sound?

When the sky outside my window turned light enough that I could plausibly call it morning, I got up, too frustrated to try to sleep any longer.

The dormitory floor was quiet, all of the rooms dark except for Julianna's where a thin line of yellow snuck under the doorway. I hesitated outside it. Jules and I had never been close, and these days she seemed so broken it was hard for anyone to connect with her at all. In that moment, I wanted to talk to her anyway – to question how exactly she had managed to fight Ben – but it was obvious she didn't know either. Forcing her to talk about it would be cruel.

I stared at Zo's door instead, willing her to wake and join me. It just hadn't been the same since Ben's magic weakened our links to each other. Being so deeply connected that we constantly dragged each other in and out of sleep had been annoying, but I'd give anything to be able to see parts of Callie and Zo's dreams right now. Hell, I even missed the six of us sleeping

41

in the same room – the closeness of it. I never thought I'd hear myself say that about those damn bunkbeds.

I turned away from the girls' rooms, leaving them to their peace, and made my way downstairs to the planning room. I got half a step through the doorway before I stopped, staring.

Miss Trager sat on a chair in the middle of the room, wrapped in a blanket and sipping a coffee. A battered and dirty book lay open on her lap, and loose pages of writing surrounded her, all of it scrawled in red ink. When I say they surrounded her, I mean *surrounded* her. Sheets of Mr Grandace's handwriting covered every inch of the floor, table, and walls. He sat on the carpet in the corner, still scribbling.

"Morning, Toby," Miss Trager said.

"Morning..." I said, not taking my eyes off Mr Grandace. "What the... What *is* this?"

Miss Trager nodded to herself slowly, as if she'd asked herself that same question several times today already. She closed the book on her lap, carefully folding a bookmark between the pages.

"It's the prophecy," she said finally. "All of it." She waved a hand at one section of floor. "Black ink is stuff that's already become clear. Red is still indecipherable."

I glanced over, noting the pages she'd indicated. There was a hell of a lot more red than black. "How did he remember all this?" I scanned the pages on the walls, taking in the strings of unconnected letters.

It didn't seem to matter that I was talking in front of Mr Grandace. His focus had 100 percent narrowed to the page in front of him.

"He read it so many times over the years. He spent years poring over it to find the six of you. He thought it could stop it – all of this." She flapped her hand in a vague gesture encompassing "everything".

I noted that she said "he" not "we". Something told me she'd given up hours ago, staying only to stop Mr Grandace going completely over the edge. Her tone was either serene or numb, I couldn't quite tell which.

"Woah..." Zo's voice sounded behind me.

I turned to see her in the doorway, staring just like I had. She stepped towards me, and linked her arm through mine, as if she needed an anchor to avoid being swamped by the words. Fragments of her thoughts rushed through my head, our connection sparking back into life now she was awake. Her internal narrative amounted to much the same as what I was thinking – this was amazing and terrifying, and perhaps we should be concerned for Mr Grandace's mental health.

He raised his head, as if I'd said that aloud. "Can you read any of it?" he asked.

Miss Trager glanced around but made no effort to get up and properly look at the pages. To be fair, she'd probably been staring at them all night.

Zo and I looked at each other, then she let go of my arm to wander towards one of the walls of red text. I did the same, taking the other side of the room. Given I'd never been able to read any of the prophecy, even when it was written in Sammy's original script, the likelihood of me deciphering any of this was low. Honestly, I wasn't sure this would work for any of us. I stared at the lines of text anyway, willing them to turn into proper words.

"The girl will know only that her mother died, and her grandmother raised her..."

I whipped around. Zo stood at the wall, her finger tracing along lines of Mr Grandace's scrawl. Miss Trager's head shot up too, and we both converged on Zo.

"You can read it?"

Zo nodded. A flush of excitement rose up inside me.

"The magic will be in her," Zo continued. "And when the time is right, she will..." she trailed off, squinting. "I can't read the next bit."

"And when the time is right, she will defeat him," Miss Trager murmured. She closed her eyes, remembering. "She will live sixteen summers before magic finds her, and on her seventeenth birthday, the sky will burst into fire, and it will begin."

The excitement I'd felt a moment earlier crashed down, hard. We'd already read that, and it had happened months ago. Well, most of it at least. The fire at Callie's birthday had been the start of everything going wrong.

"Why does it have to do that?" I slammed my hand against the page on the wall. "Why does it keep showing us the same things, when they don't help?"

Mr Grandace shook his head. "No, this is a good thing, Toby. Don't you see?" He got up, gesturing around at the pages. "We can still read it. I was scared it wouldn't work without the actual book, but we can still decipher Sammy's words—"

"No, we can't!" I grabbed one of the sheets of paper, pulling it from the wall. "We just get the same things over and over. It doesn't mean anything!"

I raised the page, ready to tear it in two. Zo and Miss Trager grabbed my wrists. Waves of colourful magic spewed out from Miss Trager as she tried to force me to calm down.

"Don't do this, Tobes," Zo said. There were no colours from her, only sparks which burned my skin, but I didn't let go. "You know you'll regret it."

I did, but it would feel so good to be destructive right now. She squeezed my arm, and the fight rushed out of me.

"I'm sorry," I told her.

"I know. It's okay." Miss Trager pulled gently on the page. I didn't release it. I wasn't sure why, but I couldn't quite let go yet. Almost as if in answer to that unspoken question, something shifted on the page.

"Woah..."

The letters rearranged themselves, blurring and reshaping into something different.

Miss Trager's hand slipped from my wrist to my arm. "What is it? What can you see?"

The words appeared one at a time. "They must... break the connections, and it... must... end in... flames."

Mr Grandace grabbed a black pen. "See? It's working. We've never read that bit before."

I took a breath, bubbles of hope rising inside me. But then I caught sight of Miss Trager's face.

"Except that's already happened, hasn't it?" I asked. "You and Sammy broke the connections, and..."

Miss Trager winced. I trailed off, not wanting to make her feel worse.

"It's okay, Toby," she said, her voice tight. "It's still useful. That's a bit we hadn't read before." She pulled another sheet from the wall. "Try again. See if you can read anything else."

I took the sheet from her, but the bubbles of hope had well and truly popped. The strings of letters on this sheet remained gibberish. I shook my head. Zo handed me a third piece of paper. Immediately the red text swirled.

"Everything... good... comes in... cardboard."

I looked up at the others, but silence greeted my words. That was... not helpful.

"Excellent!" Mr Grandace grabbed another sheet of paper, writing that down in black ink. "Now we're getting somewhere."

Zo and Miss Trager exchanged a look but didn't stop him. Fuck, I was useless. The only time I'd ever been able to read anything from the prophecy, and it was something so utterly pointless, I couldn't even be sure I'd got it right.

"Keep looking!" Mr Grandace said. "There's sure to be more."

Zo and Miss Trager glanced at each other again, then slowly turned back to the walls. They did as they were told, eyes scanning the pages for anything that jumped out, but I could tell their hearts weren't in it. Neither was mine.

"I can't," I said. "This is fucked. We should be out there looking for her, and you all know it."

Zo sighed. "Toby..."

I didn't wait for her to finish. I turned and left the room, heading back to the dorm. At least there, I didn't have to pretend my failures were helping anyone.

ZO KNOCKED ON MY BEDROOM door later that afternoon. I felt the warmth of her magic and the edges of her thoughts through the wall.

I'd spent the day in my room, moping, pacing, and trying to plan some great rescue where I could race in and drag Callie out of Ben's clutches. So far, I'd been thwarted by one pretty big problem – I had no idea where she was.

The humming I heard when she was close helped, but it only worked in a certain proximity. Much as I wanted to, I couldn't wander the entire city listening for it. If she was even still in the city, of course.

I didn't answer Zo's knock, and eventually she popped her head around the doorway. "You sulking?"

I rolled my eyes. "I'm not sulking."

She made a face that made it clear she didn't believe me. "I brought you some food," she said. "Guessing your pride didn't let you come out for snacks."

My stomach rumbled as if in response, the traitor. Zo grinned and held out a plate. In the centre was a sandwich, with a necklace of alternating red and green grapes around the edge. I popped two of them in my mouth, my mood instantly lifting at the promise of a blood sugar hit.

"Thanks. You're a good friend."

She shrugged. "Miss Caraway made it, I just volunteered to bring it up. No one else wanted to deal with Hangry Tobes." She grabbed one of the grapes and bit into it.

She sat down on the end of my bed, and I pulled myself upright to join her, folding myself into cross-legged position.

"For what it's worth, I agree with you," she said. "We can't sit around trying to read that nonsense. We need to get out there looking for them."

"So, why didn't you say anything?"

"Because *they're* not going to agree with you. There's no point arguing."

"We can't just leave her there, Zo."

"I know, I know."

Callie's image kept appearing in my mind. She'd been so thin, so desperate looking.

Zo studied my face and chewed on her lip. I couldn't quite catch the thoughts that ran through her mind. She had a song in her head – perhaps as a cover to hide her thoughts, or maybe just an earworm. I had this stupid feeling that I *missed* her. She was right there in front of me, not lost like Callie, but the closeness we'd once felt was absent.

It wasn't like I wished things could go back to the way they were, because they had never been good. We'd been prisoners at the school, even though we hadn't known it, and then everything had gone so badly wrong once we left. I wanted life to be the way it felt like it should have been. Magic *should* have been easy; *our connection* should have been easy. And most of all, Callie should have been here.

"Thing is..." Zo said quietly. "I think I might know where they are..."

I jerked, sending the grapes rolling off the plate and onto the floor. "What?"

"That thing you read – the bit about the cardboard – I think I know what it means."

"What?!" Everything good comes in cardboard? How could that mean *anything*, let alone be the answer to finding Callie?

Zo hesitated. She picked up one of the escaped grapes and squished it between her fingers.

I grabbed it off her, dumping it back on the plate. "Zo, you can't just say something like that and then not tell me. Where is she?"

Zo shook her head. "Eat something first. I'm not dealing with you when you're all low-blood-sugar grumpy."

"Zo!" The edge to my voice probably didn't help my case.

She stared at me, her eyebrows raised. I wanted to throw the food at her more than I wanted to eat it, but I picked up half of the sandwich, shoving the whole thing in my mouth in one go.

Zo made a face. "Classy."

"Just tell me," I said around the stodge of bread.

"Can I trust you not to do something stupid?"

I groaned. "Zo, seriously?" I swallowed the last of the sandwich, fighting back the urge to cough.

She shook her head slowly, a decision flickering behind her eyes. "I'm not going to tell you where she is."

I opened my mouth to protest, but she held up a hand, indicating she wasn't finished. "But I will go with you."

My automatic response was to refuse. It was one thing for me to put myself in danger, but it was quite another to drag Zo into it with me. She shrugged, almost like she didn't care either way.

"Take it or leave it, Tobes. Either we go together, or I tell Miss Trager and Mr Grandace what I know, and they sit on it for months like everything else."

Zo leaned back on her elbows and picked up another grape. She chewed on it, her expression thoughtful, but as far as I could tell there was nothing but that song in her head.

I knew her. If she said she wasn't going to tell me, she wouldn't; there was no getting around it. I didn't want to think about our only lead going to Miss Trager and Mr Grandace, who would indeed do absolutely nothing.

I nodded, slowly. "Okay," I said. "But if anything happens, you let me take the fall, yeah?"

Zo gave a snort. "Naturally." She got up from my bed and started towards the door.

"Um... excuse me? Aren't you forgetting something?"

Zo looked back, raising her eyebrows. "I already said I'm not telling you. You think I trust you not to run off during the night? We know how that played out last time."

"I'm not Callie."

"Yeah, but you're just as stupid when it comes to rescuing her." Zo gave a stretch, calm and casual as always. "We'll leave in the morning. Try not to think too much about it. We don't want the others getting wind of it."

The song she'd been singing rose up again in her thoughts, blocking out everything else. I suspected I'd be hearing it from her all night.

"In the morning," I echoed.

Zo reached out and squeezed my hand. I squeezed back, pact made. She shut the door quietly behind her. I turned back to the food she'd left me and bit into the other half of the sandwich, stopping to chew it this time.

The last time Zo and Callie had seen each other, Zo was mad at Callie. For a while, I'd thought that might make Zo less motivated to help find Callie, but honestly, I think it was part of what fuelled her. We all had amends to make – we all wanted to fix the things that had been broken. And for the first time in months, I had a spark of hope that we might be able to do it.

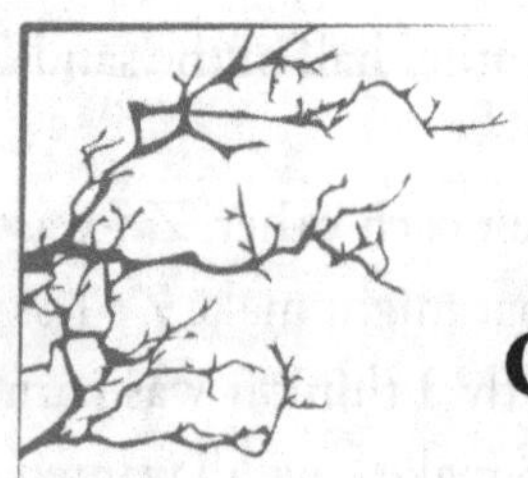

Chapter Six

Callie

Ben's lurking figure reappeared that afternoon. We all felt him before we saw him. A tightness rushed through the room that made us all sit up straighter. Mosby raised his head from my lap to growl, and the hairs on my arms stood on end, all senses tingling, ready for an attack.

We were back sitting in the staffroom again, but the atmosphere was easier than this morning. Joe and I had even exchanged a few words. Nothing of consequence of course, but it was better than the awkward attempts at avoiding each other's eyes we usually did.

Ben's entrance plunged us back into silence. He limped into the room, moving stiffly. "Did you leave me any food, Clo?" he asked.

God, he was an arrogant asshole, expecting her to cook for him after everything he'd done.

Chloe just shrugged. "On the bench."

I'm pretty sure the only thing on the bench was my half-eaten plate of eggs, and the thought of Chloe feeding him my gross leftovers gave me more pleasure than I cared to admit. I saw a flicker of recognition on Elijah's face too. I avoided looking at him in case I laughed.

Ben picked up the plate and ate a forkful of the eggs. He grimaced at the taste but ate another bite anyway. He came over, sitting on the arm of Chloe's chair.

I always had a hard time reconciling his physical presence with the looming figure in my mind. His power felt huge – overwhelming – but the man in front of us was old beyond his years. His eyes were sunken, and his shoulders hunched. He'd been tall once, that much was obvious, but his body had withered down, shrinking him as his spine compacted.

"Can either of you cook?" he asked, looking at me and Elijah.

Elijah's jaw tensed, and I reached over Mosby to grab Elijah's arm before he did something stupid like try to hit Ben.

Be silent.

Be still.

Mosby licked Elijah's hands as if he understood the risk and wanted to soothe it too.

"Fuck, you're an asshole." Chloe shoved Ben off her chair. "We're not your slav—" she cut herself off, probably remembering we *were* in fact his slaves.

Ben's brow creased, but he didn't yell at her. If Joe or Elijah had said anything like that, they probably would have landed themselves a magical blow to the chest. I'd seen Elijah laid out enough times in our first few weeks under Ben's control to know how bad it could be. Personally, I'd never been brave enough – or stupid enough – to try to defy him.

But Chloe? Chloe was his sister, and she could get away with things we couldn't.

"Whatever," she said quietly. "Cook your own food if you don't like mine."

She got up and moved over to the couch beside Joe. Ben took her chair. He sat down properly and ate the rest of the eggs in silence.

I gave Elijah's arm a squeeze before releasing it. It was always hard to assess what to do at times like this. I wanted to run away – go and hide in my room or Elijah's until Ben decided he'd had enough of "company" and pissed off to wherever it was he went when he wasn't around us.

But sometimes he got mad when we did that. Sometimes he got suspicious and wanted to know what we were hiding, lashing out at us or stealing more energy just to be punitive.

Ben put his empty plate down on the floor. Mosby abandoned me to go and lick it, even allowing Ben to stroke him. I loved the mutt, but his stomach definitely took priority over loyalty.

"Are you feeling okay?" Ben asked.

I looked up. He still held the fork and twisted it between his fingers. He stared at me, the question clearly directed my way. This was new. He didn't normally care how we were coping – or perhaps he just didn't want to know the answer.

Elijah spoke before I could. "How do you think she's feeling?" he said, his voice hard. "Steal more energy from her last night, did you? Why is it always Callie? You got some fetish for teenage girls?"

I kicked Elijah's leg hard. Fortunately, Ben ignored him. He studied my face for a moment, and then his jaw unclenched enough to speak.

"I need something from you," he said, evidently giving up on the pretence of checking up on me.

Elijah made a noise in his throat, and I could already hear the snark about to spill out of his mouth.

"E, don't," I said under my breath. I didn't look at him, but I could practically feel his teeth clamp hard on his own tongue, shutting down whatever antagonistic thing he'd been about to say.

I turned my focus back to Ben. "What do you need?"

A muscle in my face twitched at the measured tone coming out of my mouth. Playing nice was to keep me and Elijah safe, I reminded myself. I could still judge Ben for his awful life choices in private.

Ben hesitated, then he reached inside his jacket, pulling out a notebook. My breath caught. Even though Elijah had told me Ben had the prophecy, it was different seeing my mother's book in his hands.

Ben held it out. "Can you read it?"

I shrugged. Honestly, I didn't know. A few phrases had become clear to me, in the two minutes I'd been allowed to hold the book, but I hadn't exactly had the chance to peruse it, what with him enslaving me less than an hour later.

I did know, however, that even if I could read every word, I wasn't going to tell Ben a single goddamned thing.

Ben stood. He moved towards me, opening the book and splaying the pages in front of me. "Try," he said.

Mosby wandered over, reaching up to sniff the book, and Elijah leaned in, peering over my shoulder. I couldn't blame him. Our whole lives had been upended because of the prophecy. Had Elijah even seen it before? I suspected he was about to be sorely disappointed. My last encounter with my mum's book had been a monumental anti-climax.

I scanned the page. Scrambled strings of letters scrawled across it. They shifted as I tried to read them, but none of them rearranged themselves into words.

I looked up at Ben, shaking my head. He grimaced, then turned the page. "Try again."

I sighed. This could stretch out for hours, if not days – Ben making me stare at the book until something became clear. Perhaps that would be a good thing, though. At least it would keep him distracted from creating more explosions.

I shook my head. Nothing on the second page became readable either. Ben turned to another. Immediately the letters swirled, forming something coherent. My eyes widened, scanning the lines before I could stop myself.

She will see the threads, and she will follow them. They will all find the way out when they untangle the web.

Ben's hand closed tight on my arm. "What is it? What did you read?"

"I..." Damn my lack of poker face. I scrambled for something I could say instead, but my mind went blank.

Threads – just like Elijah and I had been trying to regrow between us. But Ben couldn't know about that.

Ben yanked me to my feet, displacing Mosby. And suddenly everyone was moving. Chloe grabbed Ben and tried to pull him off me, but Ben shoved her back with a blast of power. Mosby started growling, then barking at Ben. Joe stepped in front of Elijah, pre-empting his attack.

Ben twisted my arm, making it burn, and the magic rope tightened around my chest, locking me in place. "Read it, goddamn it. Read it aloud!" He thrust the book into my face.

"Read it yourself!" I shoved him, and to my surprise, he stumbled backwards. He righted himself and a rush of cold ran through me.

He stepped towards me, and I dropped my gaze to the ground, making myself small.

Be silent.

Be still.

He came right up close, his eyes burning into me. My heart hammered but he made no move to hit me. Instead, he turned towards Elijah.

I gasped. "Wait..."

Ben pushed Joe aside, then took hold of Elijah's hand. Elijah's eyes went wide then blank.

"What are you doing? Leave him alone."

"I'm not doing anything," Ben said, his tone light. He stepped back.

My stomach dropped. Ben had placed his fork in Elijah's hand. Elijah lifted his arm, slowly, muscles straining against Ben's control. I looked desperately to Joe. He grimaced but made no move to help either of us.

Elijah raised the fork, pointing the tines towards his own eye. They moved closer... closer... and then suddenly jerked back.

"Okay, okay! Stop," I gasped.

Elijah froze, fork still in the air. Chloe's breath came out in a rush.

"I'll read it," I said. "Just let me..." I reached for the book. "I didn't see it properly."

Apparently, this was the right bluff. The constriction around my chest relaxed, letting me breathe. Elijah remained frozen, the threat still in place. I felt Chloe's eyes on me. I could almost hear her willing me to lie.

I scanned the page again. *She will see the threads, and she will follow them...*

I couldn't tell him that. Another section of the page swirled, letters rearranging themselves, as I scrambled for a plausible lie. Woah. This one was different. This one was...

"Callie will read of her mother's love in the prophecy," I read aloud. "And she will tell her father he is forgiven."

My voice cracked. The prophecy was a lot of things, but an "I love you" message from beyond the grave wasn't one I'd been expecting.

"Oh my god," Joe whispered.

I looked up at him. He met my eye and his whole face crumpled. For a moment, I had forgotten he was the father in question. Not that he had acted like it just now.

"Bullshit!" Ben yanked the book from my hands, hurling it at the floor. "That can't be all you read."

Elijah and Chloe both came to life, Ben's outburst breaking his hold on them. Elijah pulled me back, putting me behind him. He threw out some magic, but Ben walked straight through it, almost seeming to get stronger as it touched him.

"It is," I said. "I'm sorry." I wouldn't tell him about the threads. No matter what, I wouldn't tell him.

"You're lying. There has to be more."

The loop around me tightened, and my knees buckled. He pulled energy from me, tearing it free like strings of sinew ripped from my limbs. I groaned, the sound turning to a shiver. Spots danced in front of my eyes, and everything dissolved into blobs of colour.

Chloe grabbed me and wrapped an arm around me, as if she could protect me that way. "Stop it, Ben! She's too weak, you'll kill her."

"Maybe that will make her read the prophecy faster."

Elijah punched him, hard. "Touch her again, and I'll kill you."

Ben crumpled under the blow. He blinked, dazed, and blood spurted from his nose. Elijah raised his fist again. Ben threw out a magical blow, sending Elijah flying back. Elijah hit the floor with a crack.

"Ben, don't!" Chloe's hand flew to her mouth.

Ben stalked after Elijah.

"Please," I whispered, but it barely made a sound.

Fear flickered in Elijah's eyes. He let out a cry and folded over. His skin went pale, the colour rushing out of him as Ben took his energy. A second later, Joe doubled over too.

"Stop it, you're taking too much!" Chloe yelled.

I tried to get up, but I couldn't. Colours still danced in front of my eyes. I could see the outlines of Chloe and Elijah, but their features were gone. Ben's outline shifted, patches fading in and out. He was barely person-shaped, just a swarming mass of other people's power. I cringed away from it, horrified.

"Fireflies," I whispered.

If Chloe heard me, she didn't react. Suddenly, all I could see was magic. The ends of my severed connection with Elijah lit up, but there were more lines than that – new ones I'd never seen before. A string joined Elijah to Ben. I watched as energy slipped along it, pulled from under Elijah's skin.

Threads tied Ben to me, Joe, and Chloe, and energy leached along those too. The chord between Joe and Chloe pulsed.

Magic travelled along it in huge sucking gulps. It flowed onto Ben, through Chloe's connection to him.

"Oh my god." I blinked, hoping fresh eyes would change what I was seeing. "No... it can't be her. She can't be..." Was Chloe intentionally helping Ben steal energy?

The lines disappeared, reality settling back into place. Ben stalked towards us, slow and deliberate. Elijah forced himself upright, refusing to fold. He stood in Ben's path, ready to attack. In a fair fight, Elijah might have won. But this wasn't a fair fight. This was an ambush from a grown man pumped up on other people's magic.

I strained my eyes, trying to make the magic light up again. Panic made my vision blur. I would do as my mum had said – I would follow the threads and unravel the web if only she gave me the chance. But there was nothing – only the sound of Ben's ragged breathing as he moved towards Elijah.

Elijah's fingers tightened around the fork still in his hand. The muscles in his arm twitched, as Ben regained control.

"Don't. Please!" I yelled.

Ben's eyes flicked to me, and I tried desperately to hold them there.

"Are you ready to read the prophecy, Calliope?" he asked.

"I'll keep trying, but Chloe's right; I'm weak." It killed me to say that, because I had spent my whole life trying to be anything but. "I can't use magic when you keep draining me," I told him. "Just... just..." Just don't hurt Elijah over my lies was what I really wanted to say.

"Just let her recover," Chloe supplied. "She can try reading it again tomorrow."

Ben looked between us. Joe lay in a heap on the floor. Elijah squared off, ready to fight to the death, and Chloe and I cowered as Ben drained the life out of us.

"Tomorrow," he said. "Tomorrow, you tell me everything it says."

"Yes. I promise."

He nodded at my acquiescence then turned away. I held my breath, listening to his footsteps retreating down the corridor. I almost broke down at the sound.

Chloe grabbed my arm as soon as he was gone. "Come on." She dragged me out into the corridor.

Her touch felt like it was burning me. What had she done? What had Ben promised her to make her help him steal energy like that?

She yanked me along, not letting me stop until we reached my room.

"What about Joe?" My voice came out as a croak.

She closed the door behind us. "He'll be fine. He's always fine," she said, her mouth set into a grim line.

That wasn't comforting at all. I eyed the door. "And Elijah?"

Chloe shrugged. He would never be her priority as much as he was mine. I'd always thought Chloe seemed to care about me a little but ultimately, she was just trying to survive. If it came down to it, she'd probably let Ben skin me and Elijah alive if it meant she got out of this. Skin us alive... or drain us to death.

I glanced towards the door again. I wished she hadn't shut it.

Chloe hovered, her gaze tracing over the concrete walls. I eyed her, warily. Did she know what I'd seen? All this time, I'd thought she was a prisoner just like us, but if she was feeding energy to Ben, then...

"I saw something in the magic." My voice was hard, the words a threat.

Chloe's eyes narrowed. "What do you mean?"

I swallowed, my throat painfully dry suddenly. "I—"

Elijah opened the door. I let out a breath, all my resolve disappearing with the puff of air. What had I been thinking? You don't confront the beast alone.

Elijah crossed the room in a single stride and sank down onto my mattress, laying his head in his hands. He was pale, shaking, and sweat beaded on his forehead.

"Are you okay?" I sat down beside him and touched his shoulder gently. He flinched. How much energy had Ben taken from him?

He pulled his palms down his face, a low hiss escaping through his lips. "Are *you*?" he asked.

I didn't know how to answer that. A heaviness had settled over my chest, perhaps from where Ben had stolen energy from me, perhaps just from the knowledge that he had the prophecy and planned to use it.

"I will be," I said finally.

An image of the tines of the fork inching towards Elijah's face flashed through my head. Did Elijah know what had happened? Did he know how close he'd just come to losing an eye because of me, or had Ben's control shielded him from that?

"And Joe?" Chloe asked.

I made a noise in my throat. "Like you care."

Chloe frowned. "What's that supposed to mean?"

I stared her down for a moment, and then dropped my gaze.

Be silent.

Be still.

Why was this so much harder than it used to be?

"Cal?" Elijah squeezed my knee.

"It's nothing." I made myself flick my gaze up, briefly meeting Chloe's eye. "I didn't mean anything." This room was too small for three people.

"What did you read in the prophecy?" Chloe asked.

I shook my head. "I told you. *Callie will read of her mother's love—*"

"Not that bit. What else?"

I shook my head again. "Nothing. That was it."

Chloe narrowed her eyes. "Are you sure?"

I nodded, not trusting myself to lie convincingly. She studied my face, and something flickered in her expression. She didn't believe me.

"Fine, be like that. You're so like Ursula sometimes."

I was like Miss Trager? As far as I was concerned, I was about as different from my former teacher as you could get.

Chloe paused, as if she was expecting me to argue with her about that, then she shook her head. "I'll talk to you later then."

I was surprised to hear a hint of hurt in her voice. She was a damn good liar. If I hadn't seen her sucking energy from Joe with my own eyes, I never would have believed it. She left the room, slamming the door behind her. I slumped forward as she did, all the tension rushing out of me. I lay down, dizzy and exhausted suddenly.

Elijah was quiet for a moment, then he lay back next to me, staring up at the ceiling. "You did read something else, didn't you?" he asked.

I nodded. "And saw something. We can't trust Chloe."

A slight frown puckered between Elijah's eyebrows but otherwise his face remained blank. "Good thing I didn't trust her to start with."

I gave a half-laugh. "Never trust a Trager, eh?"

He rolled onto his side, propping his head up to look at me. "So what happened?"

Where did I start? "When Ben was stealing energy from us, I could see it." I shivered. The way the magic had taken over made me feel strange. It was like someone had changed the channel in my brain. "Only, it wasn't just him. I saw Chloe take energy from Joe. She fed it on to Ben."

Elijah frowned. "You mean she's—"

A sound in the corridor cut him off. We both froze. Elijah pressed a finger to his lips, but he didn't need to tell me to shut up. He got up slowly and walked over to the door. He inched it open a crack and peered out. "All clear," he said. "If Chloe was listening in, she's gone now."

But was it too late? Thank god I hadn't said anything about what I'd read in the prophecy.

Elijah closed the door again, pressing on it firmly until it clicked. I beckoned him over, and he sat down close to me, leaning in so I could whisper. Once again, I wished we had managed to regain our connection. Well, if I was wishing for things, I wished our connection had never broken.

I told him the whole story in whispers, pausing every time I heard even a hint of noise in the corridor.

"So we can't trust her," I said finally. "Not until we figure out why she was helping Ben."

"Agreed."

It was the first time Elijah had spoken since I started the story – not one snarky comment or interjection. I don't think I'd ever heard him so quiet.

He chewed on the inside of his lip, thinking. "Question is, do we tell Joe?" he said finally.

I hesitated. If it were me, I would want to know that Chloe was stealing energy from me, but at the same time, Joe had just stood there as Ben hurt Elijah. He hadn't even tried to stop him.

I shook my head. "No. No one else, just us."

Elijah nodded, accepting that without hesitation. Mum might have forgiven Joe, but I sure as hell couldn't. If we were going to survive this, we couldn't trust anyone.

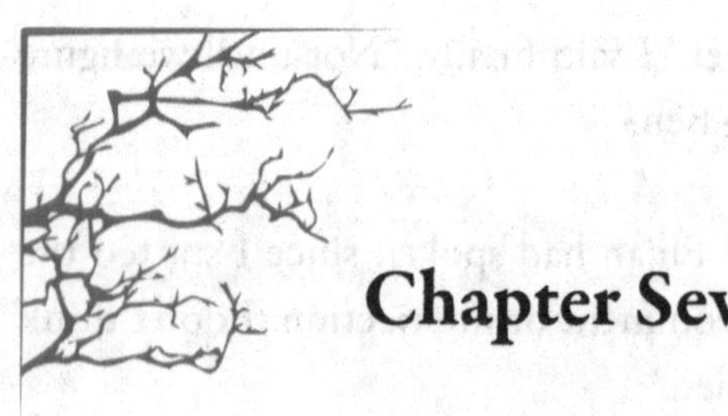

Chapter Seven

Toby

Zo kept to her word and adamantly refused to tell me where we were going. Even so, I probably could have picked up the trail after a while. Evidence of explosions became clearer and clearer. Broken asphalt lined the empty streets, as if something had been repeatedly hurled at them. The surrounding trees were all weathered, barely alive with the energy drained out of them, but vines of ivy flourished, strangling everything. The few people we saw stared blankly at us, zombies under Ben's control.

"God, what is he doing here?" Zo asked.

Probably the same thing he'd been doing everywhere – gaining energy by dragging it out of everything else. The thought made my skin crawl. If he'd done this to the trees, what was he doing to Callie and Elijah? Maybe I should be thankful for the explosions. Sucking up all the energy from big releases like that was probably the only thing stopping him from killing everything in his vicinity.

Suddenly Zo tapped my arm. "There – look!"

She pointed to an old mouldy sign out the front of an abandoned factory. *Everything good comes in cardboard.*

I shook my head, slowly. "How did you...?"

"Cardboard factory – I remembered reading it in a list of stupid slogans. I looked it up and the company went out of business two years ago. Seemed like the prophecy might be trying to lead us here."

I let out a half-laugh. "You're a genius, Zo."

"Or I spend too much time online reading stupid listicles."

I turned back to the factory. "So, how do we get in?"

Zo shrugged again. "I don't know."

"What do you mean you don't know?"

"I told you I could get you here. I didn't promise anything beyond that."

It didn't matter. This was the closest I'd gotten to Callie, other than last night. If there was even a chance I could get her out, then I had to take it. I took a step forward.

Zo grabbed my arm. "We've got to be smart about this, Tobes."

The urge to push her away and run towards the old building was strong. "What do you suggest?"

Zo studied the building for a moment, her eyes narrowing. Then she pointed to the right-hand side. "From the pictures online, there's a kind of yard around the other side. It's surrounded by a big fence, so we won't be able to get in, but..."

But we might be able to talk to Callie and Elijah. "Okay, let's go."

"You have to stay hidden, okay?"

I nodded, though everything in me wanted to barge in there, metaphorical guns – or at least magic – blazing. Instead, I let Zo take the lead. She took us around the side of the building at an agonisingly slow pace. She stopped every few steps, crouching low in the bushes, her head cocked like a rabbit's, listening.

Finally, we reached the yard, though yard was definitely an exaggeration. It was a bare stretch of dirt, maybe a couple of metres wide down the side of the building, opening out into a patch maybe four metres by two. Only the odd tuft of grass managed to survive, the rest was just bare dirt surrounded by a high chain link fence.

I dropped my head. This was pointless. There was no way we'd be able to scale the fence without being seen, not to mention the barbed wire on the top.

"Look," Zo whispered.

I raised my gaze as a figure came out of the building. He paced the length of the building, kicking the dirt in front of him.

"It's Elijah," I said.

"No shit, Sherlock."

I cracked a smile. That's just what he would have said.

We watched for a moment as Elijah continued pacing, looking more like a caged animal than anything else. He was thinner than when he'd been at the school, his cheeks drawn like Callie's. Dark hollows shadowed his eyes, and his skin was a sickly pale colour.

"Do you think I can get closer?" It took everything in me not to just run straight towards Elijah, begging him for news of Callie or a way to help them both escape.

Zo studied Elijah for a moment longer, then nodded. "I'll keep watch. But only for a minute, okay?"

I crept towards the fence. Elijah turned before I got there, walking away from me. Damn my bad timing. I waited, crouched just at the edge of the bushes.

Finally, he turned back. I felt, rather than saw, the moment he spotted me. A slight shudder went through his body almost as if he was holding in a shout. Then within a breath, he was back to pacing slowly. It took him a full minute to walk the few metres towards me. He stopped at the fence and turned, leaning back against it and closing his eyes.

"You can't be here," he said under his breath.

"I know, but..." Suddenly everything I wanted to say flew out of my head.

"You're putting her in danger," he said.

Funny how he phrased it like that – putting *her* in danger. Surely, I was putting him in danger too, but it seemed we both cared about Callie more than ourselves.

"I just want to help. Can I see her?"

Elijah tipped his head forward, rubbing his temple. He turned ever so slightly towards me. "Half an hour," he said so quietly I almost missed it. "Once it gets darker." He pushed himself off the fence and walked back into the building.

What did he say?

I started at the sound of Zo's voice inside my head. *He wants us to wait half an hour.*

Zo crept forward. "We need to get back," she whispered. "Miss Trager will notice we're gone."

"I'm not going unless I see her. Go back if you have to, but I'm not leaving."

Zo let out a frustrated sigh. She ran her hands down her face, tension tightening her shoulders. Her shoulder blades stuck out, the flesh withering from her frame just as much as Callie's. I should have noticed that before. How had I not seen how drawn she was becoming?

"We wait half an hour," she said finally. "But no more. And we move away from the fence until then, okay?"

I shuffled back from the wire mesh. It felt like wrenching a part of myself off to move away from the fence – from Callie – but Zo was right. We couldn't get caught before we had a chance to talk to her.

Zo rested her head against my shoulder, closing her eyes. She wasn't just thinner, she was exhausted. If I could honestly look at myself, I'm sure I'd see exactly the same things on my own face.

It didn't matter. We had to keep going until the others were safe.

Despite how wired I was, I dozed a little, leaning my cheek against the top of Zo's head, the feel of her spiky hair comforting and familiar.

After what felt like only minutes, she shook me awake. "She's there."

My head shot up, all stealth forgotten in my urgency to see Callie. Zo grabbed my arm, her nails digging into my bicep. I slowed at her warning, my instincts returning.

I waited as Elijah and Callie moved out of the building and away from the door. They walked in opposite directions, Elijah towards the far side, and Callie towards the fence where I'd talked to him earlier. Finally, Zo squeezed my arm, gently this time.

"Go," she whispered. "I'll keep watch."

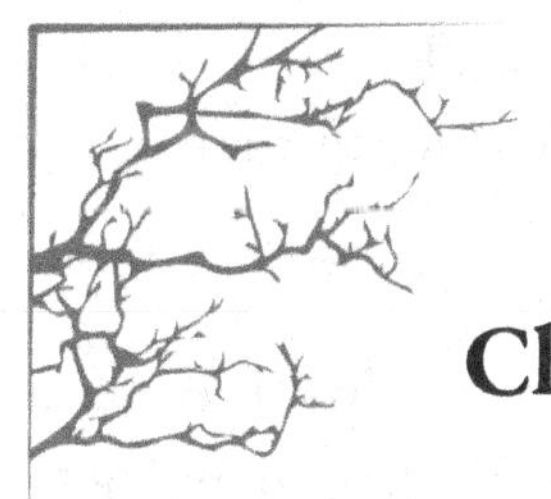

Chapter Eight

Callie

My eyes snapped open when I heard the humming.

I raised my head. It was still early, but I was already lying on my mattress, trying to sleep. Of course, there was little chance of that actually happening. Every time I started to drop off, imaginary lines of magic lit up in my head. I'd sit up to follow them, and they'd blink out, leaving me in darkness.

But the humming was something new. I scrambled to my feet, rushing out into the corridor. The discordant sounds seemed to come from everywhere, impossible to follow.

I closed my eyes, listening to the notes. They sounded familiar, some vibration my body knew but couldn't name. I let myself respond to them, humming too under my breath. I turned, almost without realising I was doing it.

A line of fireflies lit up. I waited, but they didn't blink out. One end of the thread disappeared into my stomach, anchoring somewhere deep inside me. The other led down the corridor towards the door to outside.

The humming swelled up around me, drawing me forward. I took a hesitant step. The sound tingled against my skin, almost like it was wrapping around my limbs, tiny fingers of magic latching onto me and drawing me outside.

A figure appeared at the end of the corridor.

"Toby?" His name barely made a sound, my throat refusing to believe. "Is that—"

"Cal?" Elijah called.

The humming disappeared as did the fireflies. I let out a breath, and suddenly I was desperate for air. I gasped, trying to refill my lungs.

Elijah was beside me in seconds, his hands on my shoulders. "What is it? What's wrong?"

I looked to the end of the corridor. "Did you hear that?" I asked. "The humming?"

He frowned, then slowly shook his head. I studied his face, looking for... I wasn't sure what. Signs of deception? Signs that he was the one causing the sound? I used to hear vibrations when I was around him – a pulse in the air that forced me away.

He stepped closer, but still the humming didn't reappear. He brushed the hair back from my face, staring straight into my eyes. "Are you okay?" he asked.

I shook my head. "I don't know." Was I losing my mind? Was I seeing magical threads because the prophecy had put them in my thoughts, or was there really something here trying to help us? My mother? I couldn't let myself think about that. It was too much, too confusing.

Elijah held my eye for a moment longer and then dropped his gaze. Strangely, I felt a loss at the movement. I wanted him to look back up at me.

I reached out, touching his arm. "Were you trying to find me? What's going on?"

He still didn't look up. Instead, he closed his eyes, shaking his head ever so slightly. His hands dropped from my shoulders, and he turned away, gesturing for me to come with him.

I didn't follow immediately. My skin tingled, feeling the absence of where he'd touched me. My whole body ached, and exhaustion made everything swim. The last few days, I'd felt weaker, not seeming to be able to regain my power after Ben took it. It was more than that, though. I felt like a part of me was giving up, giving in to the depression. I was so tempted to run back to my room and bury myself on the mattress. But another part of me wanted to follow the path of that magical thread.

Elijah stopped a few paces ahead of me and looked back. There was something about his manner, some urgency to it. I couldn't tell if it was a good or a bad thing.

"Okay, I'm coming."

Elijah's shoulders sagged, and his eyes flicked away from mine. I frowned. What was I supposed to make of his behaviour right now?

He turned away from me, and I padded after him, shivering a little now the adrenaline of mysterious magic had worn off.

Elijah gestured down the hallway. "Outside," he said.

The last thing I felt like doing was going and standing out in the cold. At least indoors, I could pretend I had the option to leave. Once out in that barren stretch of dirt, looking up at the fence, there was no mistaking the fact that we were prisoners. I'd almost go back to the silver bracelets locking me in place over staring at that towering wire barrier.

It was all stupid. The coil of magic wrapped around my chest linking me to Ben should have been enough to tell me

I was trapped here. I didn't know why seeing the criss-crossed mesh of the fence made it so much worse.

Elijah started down the corridor, and I stumbled into a jog to catch up with him.

"Go to the right-hand side," he said under his breath. "Right to the fence by the bushes."

I turned to look at him, but he kept his eyes on the door ahead of us. My heart started to hammer, and something tugged at my stomach as if that string of fireflies was pulling at me. We saw our classmates yesterday. We saw Toby. Could he have...?

I didn't even let myself finish the thought. It was too much to hope for. Toby wouldn't risk coming here, would he?

Elijah pushed open the door, and a wave of cool air hit me. I didn't let myself look around, walking straight over to the edge of the yard as Elijah had instructed. He didn't follow me. He wandered over to the other side, then leaned back against the fence. He folded his arms, watching me.

I strained my ears, listening with my whole body. I leaned my arms against the fence, propping my head against them, and closed my eyes. There was a strange emptiness to the night here – only man-made sounds. The absence of wildlife was deafening. Ben had dragged the energy out of all the life around here for miles. I guess I should have been grateful. It was probably the only thing stopping him from killing me.

"Callie?" Toby whispered.

I froze at his voice. I opened my eyes, slowly. At first all I saw were the droopy outlines of the bushes, but then he shifted, and like an optical illusion his figure became clear.

"Toby," I breathed, barely letting it make a sound.

I felt it – the tingling at the edges of our broken magical connection. It took everything in me to turn around, away from him. I leaned my back against the fence, pressing my palm to the wire, reaching out to him as much as I dared.

"What are you doing here?" I whispered.

"We came to get you out."

A desperate laugh slipped through my lips. "You can't."

He knew as well as I did that I was stuck here. I wouldn't have been doing the things I'd done over the last few months – causing that level of destruction – if I wasn't trapped. But still, Toby was here... He was still trying to save me despite the awful things I'd been forced to do.

"Are you okay?" he asked,

I heard him shift and I could almost imagine him reaching out to touch my palm on the other side of the fence. How could I answer that? Of course I wasn't okay. My energy was being drained by a power-hungry dictator. I'd been forced to destroy things, to hurt people, and I didn't even know why. I didn't understand what Ben wanted other than to take magic from me and Elijah. I was trapped here with my father and Chloe, and I didn't trust either of them.

"We're okay," I said finally. "Elijah is looking after me."

Toby went silent at that. I opened my eyes, staring at Elijah across the courtyard. His gaze locked on mine, but he stayed leaning back against the fence on the other side, watching, giving me space.

Suddenly Zo's voice hissed, "Toby, what are you doing?"

I couldn't help myself; I jerked around to look. Toby stood, coming forward from his hiding place in the bushes. I pressed my hand to the fence. He mirrored the movement, our hands connecting without either of us having to think about it.

I heard Elijah take a few steps forward, and I spun back, shaking my head to hold him off. "Please," I mouthed at him.

He stopped, looking to the entrance of the building. A flash of fear crossed his face. Something dropped in my stomach, and my eyes darted to the building too.

I spun back to Toby and pressed my fingers through the fence. He gripped my hand through the wire, his face just inches from mine. Threads of his magic stretched out, reaching as if they would wrap all the way around me.

"Let us get you out of here, please."

I could feel his breath on my cheek. In another lifetime, I could have kissed him.

"Toby!" Zo hissed. I could just see her crouched in the bushes behind him. She stared at me, her eyes darting between me and Toby, her fear evident.

Suddenly, Elijah was right behind me. He gripped my shoulder. "We have to go, Cal. If they catch us..."

I started to shake. Ben's magic – the rope wrapped around my chest – tightened. "Give me one minute, please."

Elijah's fingers bit into my shoulder, but I grabbed his hand. I poured every ounce of desperation I could into my grip, and I knew he felt it.

"One minute," he said. "Just one minute." He backed away a few paces, keeping himself between me and the door. I doubted it would make much difference. If Ben or one of the others came out here right now, we were done. I turned to Toby.

"I have to go," I whispered.

He shook his head. "I can't leave you here."

"You have to." I swallowed. The words felt like they were ripping a hole in my chest. I leaned towards the fence letting the edges of Ben's magic come into contact with Toby's hand. "You feel that?"

Toby drew in a sharp breath, his eyes flicking from his hand to my face.

"That's why I can't leave. And it's why you can't get caught."

He hesitated then nodded. "I love you."

I swallowed. I couldn't say it back, not when it meant he would risk himself to get me out. "And that's why you have to leave me here."

His face fell. Zo shifted forward, reaching for Toby's hand. "Come on Toby. Please?"

Toby didn't look at her, keeping his eyes locked on mine. "Are you sure you're safe here?"

A lump stuck in my throat. I looked back at Elijah.

He took a step forward. "I can protect us," he said. "But only if you leave."

I wanted to cry, but I couldn't. The only way for Toby to stay safe was for him to believe that I already was.

"I hear humming," Toby said. "When we get close. Every time, I know when you're near."

I froze. Elijah pulled me away, but I grabbed the fence hard. "Humming? You're sure?"

Toby nodded. "It's you, isn't it? Inside your head." He started to hum, the same low tone I'd been hearing for days.

"That can't be a coincidence." I looked from Toby to Elijah, but neither of them knew what I was talking about. We were still connected. Somehow, the magic still had us joined, even if we couldn't feel it. Was that why I'd seen that thread? Was that what the prophecy was trying to tell me about?

Zo tugged on his sleeve. "Please Toby. We have to go."

She pulled him back a pace. He kept his hand pressed to the fence. Elijah's arm slid around me, pulling me away too. I pressed my hand to Toby's.

"We'll figure it out, I promise," he said. The ends of his magic stretched out as he spoke, no coaxing needed. They wrapped around mine, and I shivered at the sensation. Suddenly my magic didn't feel so alien to me.

Toby's eyes went wide. "Did that just…?"

I didn't dare breathe. For months Elijah and I had tried, and nothing. But maybe… just maybe it would work with Toby. Fireflies appeared, swarming over our linked hands. They didn't burn, the sensation warm like sunshine.

Callie? he said inside his head.

Yes. I hear you.

He grinned, and sobs rose in my throat. I closed my eyes, forcing myself to remember everything. The threads… Chloe stealing Joe's magic… every piece of destruction we'd caused over the last few months. He had to know all of it.

"Elijah… Callie!" Joe shouted from inside.

My head snapped towards the door. Footsteps thundered down the corridor, coming towards us.

Toby sucked in a sharp breath. "Did you just show me—"

Another shout from inside cut him off.

"Go!" I hissed at the same moment Elijah yanked me away from the fence. Zo broke into a run, dragging Toby with her. I moved with Elijah, going back inside, not daring to look back.

I love you, I said inside my head. I wasn't sure if I wanted him to hear it or not.

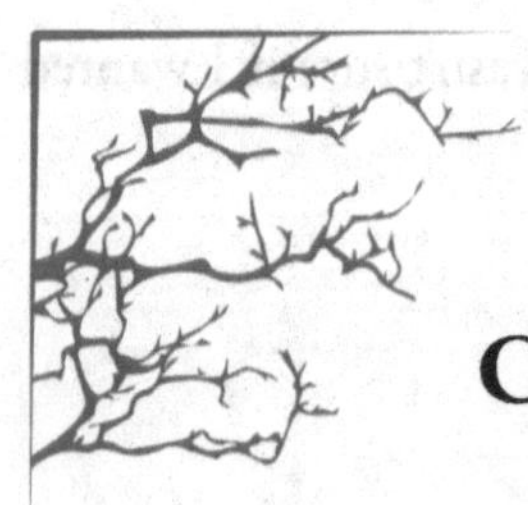

Chapter Nine

Toby

Zo didn't let go of me until we were back inside the school. I shrugged her off once we were through the doors, in the main foyer.

"You didn't have to do that," I snapped at her.

"Oh, yeah? Would you have left if I hadn't made you?"

I started up the stairs to our rooms without looking back at her.

She followed after me. "That's what I thought."

My head pounded, trying to make sense of all the new information Callie had shared. The images she'd passed to me felt like memories, but they made me nauseous to watch. What had she gone through the last few months? What had I left her to go through now?

I turned at the landing, starting on the second flight of stairs. Zo followed at my heels, and I increased my pace, trying to get away from her. She would have seen it all in my thoughts, of course, but it wasn't the same for her. She didn't care about Callie like I did.

Honestly? If Zo hadn't dragged me back here, I would probably still be outside the fence. Or, more likely, I'd be inside facing Ben and the others.

"Toby..."

I shook my head. I just needed a moment alone. My hand tingled, almost itching. The memory of Callie's magic reaching out to mine was fresh, and the sound of her voice echoed in my mind. Would it hold? Were we connected like we used to be? I almost couldn't bear to hope. I needed to test it – to see if I could reach her.

"Toby, you can't ignore me forever."

I let out a frustrated noise. "Just five minutes, Zo. Can't you just give me five minutes' space?"

Asher looked up as we stepped off the stairs onto the dormitory floor. "What's going on?" He sat on the carpet outside Julianna's room, keeping guard like her personal lapdog... or perhaps warden. I couldn't help feeling Jules was just as trapped as Callie was.

I looked at Zo. She stared back, and I could feel the thoughts flicking through her head. I couldn't quite read them, but I knew she could read mine.

Don't, I said inside my head. Did Callie hear it too? The possibility made my pulse speed up.

Zo turned away from me, focusing on Asher. "We found their base," she said. "Toby talked to Callie."

Shut up, Zo! I said inside my head.

Asher's eyebrows shot up. "You went to their...? Where is it? Does Mr Grandace know? You have to—"

The sound of a throat clearing cut Asher off. Mr Grandace stepped out of the stairwell, followed by Miss Trager.

"He does now," Mr Grandace said dryly.

I grimaced, frustration building inside me. I refused to believe he had just happened to be walking past as Asher said that. They were listening in on us, I was sure of it.

Miss Trager's eyes were bloodshot, and the dark circles underneath them extended almost to her chin. Mr Grandace wasn't faring much better. His beard had gone from straggly to sticking out in all directions, giving him a bedraggled wizard look. Somehow, the dishevelment only increased how intimidating the pair looked.

Miss Trager shook her head. "Do you have any idea how dangerous that was, especially for you, Toby? Ben got to Callie and Elijah, because of the break in their connection. That's exactly the same position you and Asher are in now!"

I glanced at Asher. It hadn't occurred to me that I was putting him in danger.

"Planning room, now." Miss Trager's tone left no room for argument. Zo, Asher and I all looked at each other.

"What about Jules?" I asked, less because I was worried about her being included, more because I was stalling.

Miss Trager glanced towards Julianna's closed door. "Leave her. She's not feeling well."

Asher and Zo both looked towards Julianna's room too. She wasn't sick, she was hiding from the magic. It frustrated me how everyone let her. We all had to fight if we were going to beat Ben.

Miss Trager's face softened as she looked at Asher. "I'm guessing you weren't a part of this?" she asked. Somehow, she'd singled me and Zo out as the naughty kids. I'd be annoyed, if she wasn't right.

Asher shook his head, eyes still glued to Julianna's door. "Nah, I've been here all afternoon."

Miss Trager nodded, then her gaze hardened again as she turned to me and Zo. "Just you two then. Both of you, downstairs now."

Zo sighed and linked her arm through mine. I flinched away, still mad.

We trailed down the stairs and into the planning room. Miss Trager and Mr Grandace had made a little progress – rearranging the screeds of scrawling writing into some semblance of order. It still looked like the raving-lined den of a serial killer.

Miss Caraway stood by the far wall, pinning up the remaining loose sheets with thumb tacks. She looked from me and Zo to Miss Trager and Mr Grandace.

"I'll finish this later," she said, quickly removing herself from the room.

Dammit. I'd half been hoping we could claim we were interrupting her work, and delay this telling off for a little longer. Instead, I slumped in one of the chairs in the middle of the room. Zo moved the book Miss Trager had been reading from the seat beside me and placed it carefully down on the floor. I glanced at the title, but the whole thing was covered in ash, making it hard to read.

"Why didn't you tell us you knew where they were?" Miss Trager asked. "What on earth possessed you to go off on your own?"

"It was my fault," I said. "I made Zo come with me."

Miss Trager made a soft sound that was almost a scoff. "I very much doubt you could make Zo do anything against her will."

"Why? He made her sleepwalk." I gestured to Mr Grandace.

Everyone went quiet, and Zo shook her head slightly. "Dude..."

I slumped back in my chair. That was petty, and I knew it, but right now I felt petty. I was sick of being told what to do. They weren't my teachers anymore, and they were the ones who'd got us into this mess. I was sick of them acting like they knew what was going on when everything they did just made things worse.

Zo cleared her throat. "That cardboard thing Toby read – it was a slogan for an old factory. We went to check it out. No, we didn't tell you, but we didn't know if it was going to pan out."

Miss Trager and Mr Grandace exchanged a look. Even though they weren't connected in the same way Zo and I were, they still seemed to be able to talk inside their heads. I closed my fingers over my palm, feeling the tingle of Callie's magic.

"Did you learn anything?" Mr Grandace asked finally.

Zo and I glanced at each other. Part of me wanted to keep everything Callie had shown me to myself. Miss Trager and Mr Grandace would just sit on it, analysing it, but ultimately refusing to act on it like everything else.

Then again, Callie had shown me a lot of stuff I didn't really understand. If there was even a slight chance they could figure it out...

"She'll see the threads, and she'll follow them. They will all find the way out when they untangle the web," Zo said before I got a chance to. "Something like that at least – Callie read it in the prophecy."

I glared at her. Why was she being like this? Why couldn't she trust me to make the right choice?

Mr Grandace grabbed a pen, scrawling that out on yet another sheet of paper. He stuck it to the wall, layering it over another page. "Anything else?

Zo shrugged. "She showed Toby a bunch of other stuff, but it was too quick for me to follow. She looked really sick. I don't know if she was in her right mind."

That wasn't fair. Callie wasn't crazy. Then again, maybe it would spur our former teachers into action if they thought she was. "We have to get her out of there," I said. "There's no other option."

Miss Trager waved her hand as if I were a phone screen she could clear. "Go back," she said to Zo. "What do you mean she showed Toby?"

Zo looked at me, and I grimaced.

"We regained our connection. At least, I think we did." I raised my hand, uncurling my fingers, as if she would be able to see the end of the connection etched on my palm.

Mr Grandace grabbed it and ran his hand across mine. "Yes, I can feel it," he said. "But it's not quite as strong as last time."

That, I'd already figured out.

Miss Trager touched my hand too, more gently. "It should still offer her some protection and stabilise her magic. If she and Elijah can find a way to rebuild their connection, they may even be able to shut Ben out."

My heart hammered inside me. Had I actually done something right for once?

"And she was able to show you something?" Miss Trager asked.

I nodded. "A lot of things. I don't know if I understood them all. A lot of stuff about the threads, a lot of fireflies. That was always how she saw magic." I closed my eyes, trying to tease out the memories. "There was something about Chloe... Callie thought she was stealing magic from Joe, passing it on to Ben."

Miss Trager's head whipped up. "What?"

I shook my head. "I don't know. It was like she could see all these strings light up and energy rolling along them. She thought it was Chloe stealing magic, not just Ben."

Miss Trager got up, striding across the room. She pulled one of the pages from the wall, scanning it.

Mr Grandace followed her reading over her shoulder. "What is it. Did you read something?"

"Maybe... I don't know." She set the page of writing down and grabbed another one.

That bloody prophecy.

"Here..." Miss Trager brought the paper over to us. She pointed at a string of red letters. The words swam under my gaze, refusing to settle into anything coherent. She looked up at me expectantly.

I shook my head. "I can't read it."

She sagged visibly.

Mr Grandace patted my shoulder gently. "Don't worry about it, Toby. This is still more than we knew this morning."

"Can you read it?" Zo asked Miss Trager. "What does it say?"

"Pretty much the same thing Callie showed you, except this bit here..." she trailed off, not elaborating on what the extra bit was.

How could we even call it a prophecy when all it seemed to predict were things we already knew?

Suddenly, she strode back across the room and picked up the book Zo had placed on the floor. "Side effects of stolen magic..."

She brought the book over to the wall and picked up the piece of prophecy. She placed the page back on the wall, smoothing it out carefully, then held the book up next to it as if comparing the two texts. She mumbled to herself, too fast and quiet for the rest of us to understand. We were done getting anything coherent out of her for the day, that much was obvious.

"Anything else we should know?" Mr Grandace asked.

Zo shook her head and looked to me. I clenched my hand into a fist, balling my other hand over it.

Callie? I whispered inside my head. I held my breath, waiting for an answer. The silence stretched out in response.

"No, nothing," I said aloud.

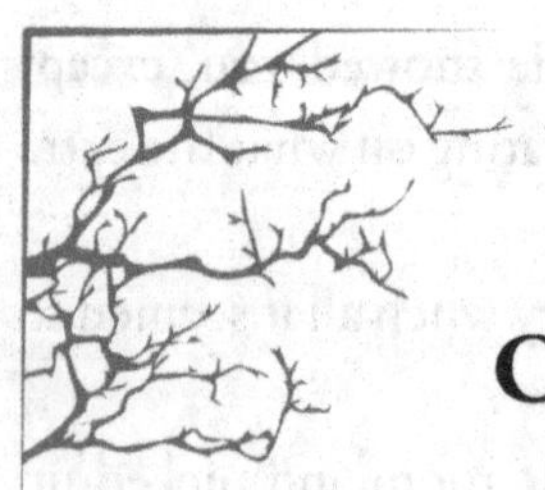

Chapter Ten

Toby

I spent the rest of that night talking to Callie in my head. I replayed memories; my favourite ones of her, and also things we had learned since she left. I gave her every single piece of information that might be able to help her. I had no idea whether she could hear any of it, but I had to try.

Zo would be able to hear it, of course. I was probably massively pissing her off, but I didn't care.

At some point, I fell asleep and dreamed about Callie, Elijah and the others. The dreams felt almost as real as the memories she'd shown me. I woke several times in a cold sweat, blinking to clear the images of buildings exploding, their zombie-like owners stuck inside as Ben's control froze them in place.

Before it was even light out, Miss Caraway woke us, telling us Mr Grandace wanted us up and ready for "training". I dragged myself out of bed to shower and eat breakfast.

"You still pissy with me?" Zo asked as we sat down in the dining room.

I shrugged. "Are you?"

She shook her head. "Nah, but if you could have less involved dreams tonight, that would be great."

"You saw that?"

Zo nodded, stifling a yawn. "You think it's coming from Callie?"

"I don't know... I hadn't thought of that."

"You spent all last night trying to show her stuff. You think she's not obsessing about you enough for you to end up with her dreams? Even without the *actual* connection, you two are connected."

That made a lot of sense, but I wanted to vomit at the thought. What she'd shown me voluntarily had been bad enough. If she'd lived through everything I'd seen last night, I had no idea how she was still standing.

"Alright," Mr Grandace called. "Five minutes, then I want all of you in the foyer ready for training."

Zo rolled her eyes, but we both got up to put our dishes in the kitchen. Every time Mr Grandace started down this track, a little niggle of irritation tweaked my stomach. Training. What were we training for? To fight Miss Trager's siblings and the others, obviously, but training implied he had a plan on how to achieve it. Why did he keep refusing to tell us what it was?

It didn't matter. I had a plan of my own now. I just had to keep Zo out of my head long enough to put it into place.

Mr Grandace had us run up and down the stairs in the foyer for a while. Usually Miss Trager joined in, helping with the drills, but she'd left the dining room after breakfast, heading towards the old burnt-out library. It was always a sign of a bad day when she ended up in there.

When we first did training sessions, I thought the running part was pointless – I wanted to get into growing our magic. Now, I was starting to see the value. I'd done more running chasing after Callie in the last couple of months than I had in the last few years. Ben and the others weren't going to just stand there and let us try to overthrow them.

Today especially, the running would come in handy.

"Okay, let's try practicing some magic skills," Mr Grandace said.

Julianna whimpered and turned away. I rolled my eyes. My patience for her magic-aversion was wearing thin.

I expected Asher to rush over and start coddling her like he usually did, but instead he walked over to me. "How about we pair up today?" he asked.

I blinked. I glanced over to the side of the foyer, where Julianna now sat, staring at the tiled floor. Her hair was loose, and it hung greasily over her face. Zo followed my eyeline, and her eyebrows pinched together.

"Yeah, I'll work with Jules today," she said.

Asher nodded. "Yeah... okay. That's a good idea."

I got the feeling they'd planned this, given Asher very rarely thought anything Zo did was a good idea. Whatever. It worked in my favour. If I paired with Zo, she'd be stuck to me like a limpet, but with Asher as my partner, I might actually get a chance to sneak off.

I turned back to him. "What did you have in mind?"

He gave me the briefest of smiles. "I thought we could go outside. Maybe try something bigger?"

I grinned. That was perfect. Not in the magical sense – "bigger" magic wasn't exactly in my wheelhouse – but the idea of getting out from under Zo and Mr Grandace's watchful gazes appealed.

Out in the garden, Asher sat down on the ground, picking up a couple of rocks. I frowned. When he said he wanted to do bigger magic I wasn't picturing cobbling together stones. He closed his eyes, holding them in his hands. They started to grow and to multiply.

I picked up a pebble of my own. I closed my eyes, pouring my magic into it. Slowly, it warmed and then started to expand.

"Nice one, man!" Asher said.

I smiled faintly at the praise. Mine hadn't doubled in size in the same way as Asher's had, but it had gone from a pebble to... a slightly larger pebble. It was a start at least.

"Will this work with other stuff?" I asked.

He shrugged. "Should do. You want to grab some things and try it out?"

Perfect. Asher could have levitated anything he wanted over to us, but I didn't point that out. "Yeah, man," I said. "I'll be back in a sec." Or not.

I made a show of collecting a few sticks, then wandered around the side of the building. The main gates to the property were closed – of course they were, things could never be that easy – but what was the use of magic if you couldn't scale a few fences with it?

I found a spot hidden from the house by the trees. The fence was old, made up of creaking metal railings that didn't seem like they'd hold my weight, but that was where the magic came in.

An image of Callie and I falling from the tree as we'd tried to escape the school flashed through my head. Maybe we should have kept going. Sure, we'd saved our teachers and classmates that night, but only for a little while. My choice to join our magic together had hurt them just as much as it had helped.

I took a firm hold of the fence, then braced my foot against it, pushing myself up.

A hand slammed down on my shoulder. I gasped and let go of the fence, falling back onto the person behind me. We hit the ground hard.

"Shit!" Asher yelled.

I rolled off him. "Sorry!" I scrambled to my feet. "I thought you were Mr Grandace."

Asher groaned. "Nah, I'd never have a beard like that."

That was actually pretty funny for Asher. He pulled himself up to a seated position and brushed the dirt off his back. "What were you doing?"

I glanced awkwardly at the fence. "Would you believe I was trying to get higher to gather sticks straight off the trees?"

"About as much as I believe you wanted to work with me to improve your magic skills." He sniffed, wrinkling his nose, then looked from me to the fence. "I'm not Mr Grandace," he said slowly. "But I still can't let you go running off by yourself, Tobes."

I huffed out a breath that was almost a laugh. "Yeah, I get it."

If the situation had been reversed, I probably would have been saying the same to any one of my classmates. I wouldn't let them go off to face danger on their own – I'd been furious when Callie had run off all those months ago... but what choice did I have?

"I can't just leave her there."

Asher nodded, slowly. "I know, man. It sucks. I feel like an asshole for leaving Elijah there."

That wasn't the same thing. Honestly, I wasn't even sure if Asher liked Elijah, he just felt guilty.

Asher tilted his head towards the house. "Come on." He got to his feet, walking a few paces before looking back.

I hesitated and glanced at the fence again. If I was fitter, perhaps I could have done some kind of parkour leap and vaulted over the fence to freedom before Asher had a chance to catch up. Instead, I turned away and trailed after him.

He waited for me to reach him, then started walking again, keeping pace with me. "Tell me about what you saw," he said.

"What I saw?"

He kicked a heavy stone along the ground in front of us. It was one of the ones he'd enlarged, its edges unnaturally perfect and smooth. "When you went to their hideout. Describe it to me."

I shrugged. "We didn't see much. There was a big fence around the building, and just this kind of dirt yard. Elijah came out, and he went and got Callie. We talked for a little while."

We rounded the corner to the main gardens. Zo had brought Julianna outside. They walked slowly around the circumference of the lawn, their arms linked. So much for magic practice. It didn't look like they were using any power whatsoever.

Asher turned towards me, stopping suddenly. He stared dead into my eyes. "Jules isn't going to last much longer like this," he said.

Immediately, I felt like an asshole. I was getting annoyed at Julianna for not wanting to use magic, but in all honesty, she was probably just as unwell as Callie was. She was crumpling before our eyes, and Mr Grandace and Miss Trager were just watching it happen.

"Do you remember where to go?" Asher asked.

I frowned. "What do you mean?"

"Zo said she didn't give you the address, but do you remember where to go? To get to the factory?"

I nodded slowly. Asher's gaze dropped to the stone at his feet. He picked it up and tossed it lightly back and forth as if it weighed nothing.

"Let's go," he said suddenly. "Tonight. Let's get Callie and Elijah out of there."

"How? Ben has them wrapped in magical ties."

Asher shrugged. "Magic can be broken. We've proven that already." He tossed the stone into the air. It arced upwards, then slowly started to drop. Asher flicked his hand, and the stone burst in mid-air, showering us both with a cloud of dust.

He turned back to stare at Julianna. "It's my fault that Elijah ran off that night." Asher didn't look at me, his focus entirely on Julianna. "I was connected to him. He was my Geminus pair, but I didn't even try to help him. I can't let this shitshow keep destroying Jules," Asher said, his voice grim. "She needs to be able to go home."

It wasn't Asher's fault. Callie had run off too, and I should have been the one to stop her, but neither of us had been able to do anything.

The Geminus pairs had been a mistake; we were all connected to each other, both with the natural field of magic between us, and the links that I had created to try and stabilise it. If only it had worked – we probably would have been able to keep Ben out – but that broken link between Elijah and Callie had caused so many problems. The irony was, now they were more connected than any of us. I couldn't help but feel a pang of jealousy about that.

I closed my hand over the fragile connection between me and Callie.

"So, tonight?" Asher asked.

I nodded. "Tonight."

One way or another, we would get Callie and Elijah out of there.

WE WAITED UNTIL THE others fell asleep, and then crept out. I'd underestimated how dark it would be, but Asher seemed to have some sixth – or perhaps magical – sense for moving around in the limited light.

We made it outside before anyone challenged us, but a voice hissed from behind us, as we were crossing the gardens.

"What are you doing?" Julianna's silhouette appeared in the open doorway.

Asher turned back, his face stricken, and I sighed. There was no way we would be leaving now.

Zo pushed past Julianna and strode across the grass towards us. "What the hell, Toby? Did you really think we wouldn't notice you were gone? We're connected to you, for god's sake!"

"Please, Zo..." I didn't know what to say. She knew how much we needed to do this. I could barely function knowing that Callie was out there under Ben's control.

Zo shook her head and looked to Asher. "Toby I get, but what's your excuse? You're supposed to be the disgustingly level-headed one."

Asher clenched his jaw, then his eyes flicked towards Julianna, still standing in the doorway. She looked so small, almost waiflike. I could practically see through her.

Zo followed his gaze, staring at Jules for a moment. *Stupid boys losing their heads over girls,* she thought. *Thank god I'm a lesbian.*

I caught myself before I pointed out that she had also come pretty close to losing her head over Julianna. Zo raised her face to the sky, breathing deeply as she studied the stars.

"We just want this to be over," Asher said quietly. "We need it to be."

Zo closed her eyes, but she nodded slightly. "When this is all over, I'm moving to Latvia. That ought to be far enough away. I'll meet some nice girl, settle down, and never think about any of you again."

Asher and I looked at each other, then back at her. I inched backwards as if we could sneak off before she noticed. Finally, she opened her eyes and levelled her gaze.

"Come on, then," she said.

"Huh?"

"I know I've got balls-all chance of stopping you, so I guess I'm coming too. Someone's got to look out for you muppets."

Asher huffed out a breath, but I couldn't tell whether it was in irritation or admiration. He glanced back at Julianna.

"I'll stay here," she said quietly. "Cover for you if I can."

I didn't know how much use Julianna would be in covering for us. She shivered in the night air, as if the lightest breeze would knock her over. Asher wavered. He took a step towards her, but she shook her head. She reached out as if she would take his hand, though she was too far away, then dropped it to her side. "Go. End this."

Asher's whole body seemed to steel as if in response to her words, and he nodded once. He turned back to me and Zo. "Let's do this."

Chapter Eleven

Callie

Elijah slipped into my room that night. "You awake?" he whispered.

"Yeah." I'd been asleep earlier in the night, and strange dreams about Toby, Miss Trager and my mother had filled my head. In them, I saw my mother's death over and over. She stood at the top of a staircase, then she and Miss Trager snapped the chord of magic between them, causing an explosion. Again and again the image played, and each time I felt more like I'd actually lived it.

Elijah pressed a finger to his lips. "Ben's roaming like a drunk toddler tonight," he whispered, then tilted his head towards the corridor. "Let's go somewhere he can't hear us."

I pulled myself out of bed and followed after Elijah. A part of me had been hoping he was waking me because Toby was back, but a bigger part of me hoped my former classmates stayed far away. The last thing we needed was for Ben to start stealing their magic too.

Elijah led me down the corridor to the warehouse part of the factory. Mosby lay asleep outside Joe's room. He thumped his tail when he saw us. I pressed my finger to my lips, and he laid his head back down.

We didn't often come down to the warehouse – the space was full of old machinery, not to mention stacks of rotting cardboard. We slipped in behind a pile of it, hoping it would keep us hidden if Ben came looking.

"So?" Elijah asked, once we were settled.

I sniffed. The mould from the piles of cardboard had my sinuses streaming already. Maybe this wasn't worth the cover it provided. "So... what?"

The air around Elijah seemed charged somehow, almost like it used to be. It didn't completely push me away – if I'd wanted to, I could have moved right in close to him – but if I listened hard enough, I could almost hear a hint of that pulsing hum. He didn't speak. Instead, he chewed on his lip, watching me.

"Spit it out, E," I said finally.

"Huh?"

"Whatever it is you're debating saying."

He let out a half-laugh. "You know me too well." He sounded almost bitter when he said that.

He touched his right palm, and tiny threads of power lit up. The hum I'd thought I could hear went from a hint to a rumble. Strings of fireflies rose, reaching for me.

"You managed to connect to Toby's magic, didn't you?" He stared at his hand instead of me, though I could tell he was aware of every movement I made.

"I..." I shook my head. Guilt trickled through me, though I wasn't sure why. "Yeah. I think so, at least. It happened automatically, but it's not as strong as it used to be. I haven't been able to hear him since he left."

I should have tried to strengthen the connection – made sure I could actually use it – when Toby was in front of me. But in that moment at the fence with Toby, all I'd been able to think about was how much I'd missed him.

"Everything was so rushed," I added.

Elijah nodded. He looked up at me, his eyes tracing my face, searching for... something.

"And you and I can keep trying," I said. I didn't know why, but that felt like a lie.

Elijah made a soft noise in his throat. I dropped my gaze, my cheeks heating.

"Perhaps with all of us joined we'll be able to break Ben's hold," Elijah said.

I couldn't help hearing that as a jibe. If I hadn't broken our connection, maybe Ben would never have been able to take hold of us in the first place.

"If we can figure out what my mum meant about the threads, we won't even need the connections."

That was placing a lot of hope in a vague note from my mother's notebook. Then again, what else did we have to place hope in?

The silence hung between us for a long moment. Or *not* silence as it was. Elijah moved towards me, and the humming rose in a wave like feedback from a microphone.

"Do you know why?" he asked.

"Why what?"

He hesitated, then reached out, touching my palm. "Why you can connect to Toby and not me?"

Something squeezed inside my chest. The way he said that, it was like he thought I'd chosen this, but his and my magic had always repelled each other. I had no control over it. At least... I didn't think I did.

"I don't know," I said finally. "I guess Toby was the first person I trusted at the school." He had been one of the first people I'd trusted full stop, but that was beside the point. "Maybe that made the magic stronger."

"You don't trust me?" Elijah's eyes flicked up to mine.

"I didn't say that." I hadn't said it, but did I mean it? I honestly wasn't sure.

"But you don't." Elijah looked away, closing off from me.

"I didn't say that!" I said again. "But I mean, back at the school—"

"I was behaving like an ass, I know. I wasn't worth trusting. But I've changed. You see that, right?" He ran a hand through his hair, the gesture stilted and jerky. He was breathing fast, and his eyes telegraphed enough pain that I couldn't hold his gaze.

"Yes," I said. "I know you've changed."

"But not enough."

"I didn't say that." I was going to be repeating that same mantra all night. I'd trusted him enough to tell him about Chloe. That meant something, didn't it?

We both fell quiet again. Even without being connected to him, I could feel what he was thinking. I could feel his desire to step closer to me, and the humming rose up almost as if in warning. He swayed towards me, and I raised a hand to stop him.

"Those flowers you gave Julianna," I said, almost before the thought had fully formed in my mind. "Back at the school – the poisoned ones. Why did you do that?"

Elijah went still. He half turned away from me and when he spoke, his voice was tight. "I didn't know you knew about that."

I swallowed. "Were you trying to hurt her?"

"No... I don't know."

"Were you jealous?" The way both Zo and Asher flocked around Julianna, it wouldn't surprise me if Elijah was in love with her too. He'd also been weirdly clingy with Asher.

He started to shake his head again, but then stopped himself. "Maybe. You don't know what it was like – before you arrived, I mean. They were all friends, but I was on the outside."

"So... you figured if they were going to reject you anyway, you'd give them a reason to do it?" I'd been there. When being small and quiet didn't work, I'd burned many a bridge trying to keep myself safe.

"Maybe." The corner of Elijah's lip twitched, fighting a grimace. "No one ever likes me, why bother trying to make them?"

"I like you."

Elijah frowned as I said that. He studied my face as if looking for deception. I stared back, trying to make my expression as open as I could. I might not have liked him at the start – might have been afraid of him even – but I cared about him now, that much I was sure of.

He reached out, hesitantly running his hand down my arm. "Would things have ever been different? If you'd met me before Toby?"

I took a breath, then let it out without saying anything. How could I answer that? What would it even matter if I did? His expression darkened at my silence.

A noise from the other room made us jump. Elijah's hand closed around my arm, his fingers biting into my skin. More thumps sounded, like a foot pounding against the wall. I scrambled up.

Elijah leaned in close, his lips brushing my ear. "We have to get back to our rooms."

I nodded. We'd been stupid to stay out this long.

We crept along the wall, aiming for the sliver of light coming from the corridor. Mosby stood outside the door to the warehouse, his tail between his legs. He pressed up against me, his head turned back to peer in the direction of the noise.

"Go," Elijah whispered. "I'll distract Ben."

I shook my head. The noise was coming from the staffroom, and light spilled out from the doorway. There was no way I'd get myself and Mosby down the corridor straight past that open doorway without Ben noticing.

Then I saw it. Strings of fireflies lighting up, leading me towards the room.

"What is it?" Elijah whispered.

"Threads," I said.

Elijah hesitated. He looked between me and the staffroom, and for once, I thought I saw fear in his expression. He turned back to look at me properly. "You're sure the prophecy said to follow them?"

I nodded. "Definitely."

"What the prophecy wants, the prophecy gets, right?"

Was that right? Every time we'd tried to do something it suggested we'd made things worse for ourselves. Perhaps my mother had been unhinged all along. Maybe the prophecy was nothing but rambles, predicting the future only in the same way magazine horoscopes did, with a lot of confirmation bias and liberal interpretation of vague statements.

Elijah slipped his hand into mine. He pulled me forward, and without thinking I was following – him and the thread. My heart hammered, several thumping beats for every step. The fireflies got brighter, and they let off a low sound. The noise swelled until it reverberated inside my head. Was this a warning? Was something trying to force me away, despite the prophecy urging us to follow? For all the power magic was supposed to hold, it really lacked in the communication department.

I squeezed Elijah's hand, reassuring myself, and he tightened his grip in response. Ben's voice came from inside the room. We paused outside the door, looking in. He'd tossed the room, furniture upended and couch cushions hurled across the floor. He rummaged in the base of the couch now, as if looking for spare change.

"Where did it go?" he said. "It's not in the book. It's not here."

He looked up. I froze, but no anger flashed in his face. He waved the prophecy at me. "I thought she put it in here, but there's nothing."

"Is he drunk?" Elijah said under his breath.

I didn't dare nod, but yes, Ben was definitely drunk.

"I just want to stop. But I can't until I get it."

"Get what?" I surprised myself by saying that. Though most people got more dangerous when they were drunk, Ben suddenly felt a lot less threatening. His movements were big but floppy, nothing intimidating about them.

"The magic! I just want it to stay. I thought if I had all of them, I'd be done, but then Sammy went and died."

I felt like he'd hit me. My mother didn't just *go and die*. He killed her. Or at least, he caused her death.

"I thought she'd put it in the book – stored it away for safe keeping, but there's nothing here." He waved the book again. The pages scrunched up under his fingers, and I cringed at the sight. As much frustration as it had caused me, the prophecy was still my one link to my mother.

I hesitated, then reached out my hand. "Can I have it?" I asked.

Ben stared at me, then slowly looked down at the notebook, almost as if he'd forgotten what it was. He held it out, swaying slightly as he did. I took it gingerly, afraid he would snatch it back at the last second, but he let me take it from him. I smoothed the pages out under my hand.

"What are you doing?" Elijah said under his breath.

I didn't reply. The book hummed now it was in my hands, but it wasn't a discordant sound like the ones I'd been hearing. This seemed familiar... welcome.

"I just want the magic to stay inside me," he said. "But it always drains away. I always have to take more."

I frowned, and I felt Elijah glance at me. Chloe had explained how she and Ben had to take energy from objects and other people to fuel their stronger magic, but she'd never said anything about it draining away.

I reached out in my mind, tentatively feeling the edges of his power. The rope around me tightened, warning me off, but I kept going. He always seemed so strong – magically at least – but there was a sort of flux to the energy around him. It flowed towards him, dragged out of me and everything around us, but there was also magic flowing away from him.

"It's leaching out of you," I said. "You really can't hold onto it."

Ben's eyes widened, and he almost smiled. "See? You get it now."

Could it be that he wasn't trying to make himself stronger, but to simply keep his own magic – his own energy – from draining away?

"Side effects of siphoning magic," he said as if quoting something.

A memory flashed through my head. No, not a memory exactly, but something from the dream I'd had. A book – Miss Trager holding it out in a room full of ash. Other memories crowded in around it, all of them too fast for me to understand.

Suddenly, the prophecy felt hot in my hands, no longer welcoming but urgently drawing my attention. I almost dropped it. *Tell me what to do*, I wanted to ask it. *Tell me how to escape this.*

In response, the humming sound swelled.

Ben's head snapped up. "What is that?"

Elijah stiffened. He could hear it too, I was sure of it.

Every last hint of benevolence rushed out of Ben's face. He rubbed at his ears, scratching the skin in front of them. "All night... All night it's been going on. I can't sleep with that noise."

Elijah pulled me back, putting himself between me and Ben, but Ben's eyes were locked on me.

"You know something, don't you? You're keeping it from me – lying, always lying, just like Chloe!" Ben's loop of magic tightened around me, draining me. I gasped, the air disappearing from my lungs.

He reached for the prophecy, but I pulled it tight against my chest. It burned there, too hot to hold, but I couldn't let go. Ben lunged forward. Elijah got to me first. He shoved me back. I stumbled, falling into the corridor. Elijah slammed the staffroom door, shutting me out, and closing himself inside with Ben.

I scrambled to my feet. Humming swelled around me, blocking out everything else. But then Elijah's voice, somehow inside my head, became clear.

Callie, run!

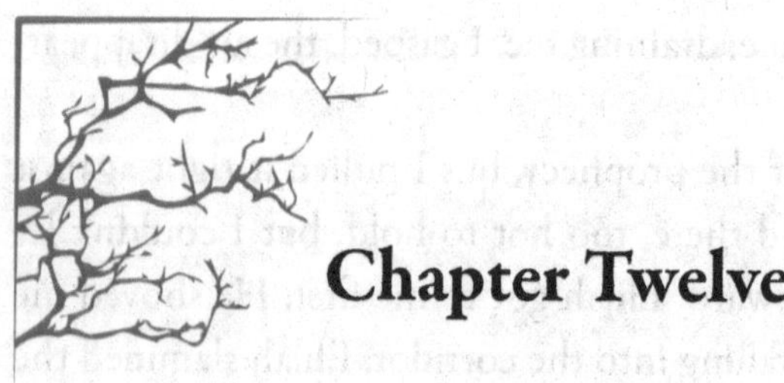

Chapter Twelve

Toby

"So, what's the plan?" Zo asked. "Scale the fence?"

I stared up at the height of the wire fence from our spot hidden in the bushes. I was embarrassed to admit that I hadn't got that far. I'd been so relieved when Asher decided that he would come with me – that he would help me get Callie and Elijah out – that I hadn't thought through what we were going to do once we got here.

Asher shook his head. "I think we can do better than that." He closed his eyes, concentrating. Zo and I looked at each other. I could practically feel her heart rate rise at the thought of doing magic so close to someone who was literally an energy vampire. Would this alert Ben to our presence?

Asher opened his eyes, a satisfied smile spreading across his face. I looked around. Nothing appeared to have happened.

He rose into a stooped crouch and scuttled over to the fence. He pushed against it gently and a piece of it swung forward like a gate.

Zo let out a breath that was almost a laugh. "Nice work, man."

Asher didn't respond to the praise. His eyes traced the building. "Can you talk to Callie?" he asked me.

Callie? I called inside my head. I counted my breaths as I waited for her reply. Nothing, not even that humming.

"It's okay, man," Asher said. "We'll figure it out."

I leaned my head back, looking up at the sky. The last few months, "figuring it out" had meant doing nothing and hoping the problem solved itself. I couldn't do it anymore.

"Fuck it," I said. I got up and ran.

"Toby! What are you doing? Stop!"

I heard Zo calling after me, but I didn't slow my pace. I ran straight inside... and then I abruptly halted. The adrenaline went out of me in a rush. The corridor was dimly lit, about half of the long fluorescent bulbs burnt out. It smelt like mould and dead things, and I was suddenly thankful for the lack of light.

The slap of feet behind me made me turn. Zo and Asher dodged through the door. "Dude, what the hell?" Zo hissed.

I shook my head. I hadn't meant to lead them into danger, but I couldn't stand out there doing nothing. Zo and Asher looked at each other again, and I could tell they were questioning my sanity. A silent conversation seemed to pass between them, then Asher turned back to me.

"I have a plan, if you don't," he said.

I don't think any words have ever brought me more relief than those ones did. He opened his backpack and took out a stack of silver bracelets.

"Here." He handed us each a pair. "Escape route home. I've got some for Callie and Elijah too. Ben won't see it coming."

"But we have to break Ben's bonds first," I said.

Asher shook his head. "Teleporting ought to snap them, right?"

I couldn't even form words; my mouth just gaped open at him. Ben had ropes of magic tying Callie to him. Yeah, maybe they would snap with the force of the teleportation magic... but what if they didn't? Visions of Callie suffocating as the bonds tightened around her filled my head.

Asher threw his hands in the air, the bracelets flashing as he did. "Well, what's your plan then? I say we jump them out of here while we can, and deal with the consequences later."

"Are you crazy?" Zo practically shouted the words. I pressed a hand to her mouth, and she shook me off. "Toby, are you actually talking about kidnapping your girlfriend?" At least she lowered her voice this time.

"Not just Callie," Asher said. "If we can, we're going to grab Elijah too. Besides, it's not kidnapping if they want out of here."

I hadn't thought about Elijah. Between the three of us, we might be able to get Callie out, even if she was kicking and screaming, freaking out about the rope, but Elijah was bigger and stronger. There was no way we'd be able to manhandle both of them.

"Do you even know what this will do to her?" Zo hissed at me.

Asher shook his head. "It doesn't matter. We have to end this. Julianna's going to lose it if we don't fix this soon, and the rest of us will be next."

"Stop saying stuff like that!" Zo shook her head. "Julianna is fine. Her only problem is you treating her like she's break-able."

I cleared my throat. "I think we're getting off track here."

"She's not fine." Asher didn't seem to register I'd spoken, his glare firmly fixed on Zo. "She can barely eat."

"She's stronger than you give her credit for," Zo said. "She was the one who stood up to Ben while you were unconscious on the ground."

Asher blinked. "She what?"

"See, she didn't even tell you because you're too overprotective."

Zo had a point. Asher was too overprotective of Jules. Wait... what about me? Was I too overprotective of Callie? Was I only avoiding pulling her out of here because of the potential risk when it might be a risk she'd *want* to take?

"I think Asher's right," I said, though I still wasn't a hundred percent on that. "We grab Callie, get her back to the school, and we deal with whatever happens once we're there."

My mouth went dry at the thought. Could this kill her? But then again, Ben would kill her if we didn't get her out.

Zo stared at me, slowly shaking her head.

"We have to," I said finally. I tried to pour everything I was thinking into the connection between me and Zo. Her face flickered through a range of emotions, reading my thoughts.

I didn't wait for her to answer, instead looking to Asher. He gave a single grim nod. "Which way?"

I glanced one way down the corridor then back the other. The building was so bare, both directions looked identical. I'd always thought the hallways of the school were intimidating, but they had nothing on this. A ping sounded in my stomach, pulling me to the right.

"This way." I set off down the corridor. "I can feel it."

"Are you sure?" Asher kept pace with me, and after a second Zo trailed after us.

"Tobes, please just think about this—"

"Elijah!" Callie screamed from somewhere behind us, cutting Zo off. Thuds echoed after the shout, like fists pounding against a wall.

Zo spun around, running towards the sound instinctively. I went to follow, but Asher grabbed my shoulder. "The magic said this way, right?"

"What?" I shook him off. "Yeah, but—"

A dog burst into a series of barks and growls down the corridor. Callie screamed again.

"It's Ben messing with us," Asher said. "Misdirection. We should follow the magic – follow the threads, like you said." He took off in the opposite direction to Zo.

My head flicked between Zo and Asher, watching both of them get further away. Which way? My head said follow Asher – go the way the magic had said. But my heart heard Callie scream, and everything else went out the window.

An image flashed in my head. Fists hitting a door, shouts and crashes coming from inside, a dog pressing against Callie's legs, his hackles raised.

I gasped, coming back to myself. *Callie? Come on, Reactive Girl. Tell me where you are.*

The ping sounded in my stomach again. *Follow the threads.* I had to trust the magic. I took off in the direction it pulled me.

I turned a corner, and the lights went out with an unnatural hiss. I froze. Solid black pressed in on me from all sides. I reached out, finding the wall and navigating along it. "Callie?" I whispered. "Please, Callie, it's me!"

The ping cut out abruptly. I stopped. What did that mean? Go back? I spun around. Footsteps thundered towards me. I raised my hands, spreading my fingers, hoping like hell my reactive magic would kick in.

"Toby?" a familiar voice said from the dark.

"Asher!" I hissed.

He raced over to me. "Did you find her? I feel like I'm going around in circles."

"No, and I lost Zo." Or, more honestly, I'd abandoned Zo.

He grabbed my arm. "Come on, let's go back the way you came."

But just as he said it, the ping hit my stomach again. Asher took a sharp inhale. He could feel something too. This time it was stronger, more urgent, jerking me forward.

Asher's hand tightened on my arm. "In there?" he asked.

"Yeah." We both reached out, feeling the shape of the door in front of us. I strained, trying desperately to sense something through my connection with Callie.

"Open the door," he said. "I'll grab her."

I hesitated, all the earlier doubts rushing back. "What about Zo?"

"You worry about getting Callie home. I'll get me and Zo out."

He shoved me towards the door, and before I even registered what I was doing, I'd opened it. It was pitch black. I heard a gasp, and then footsteps running towards me. I couldn't see anything, but magic swirled around me, taking over. My limbs moved against my will. I grabbed Callie around her waist. She shrieked and her hair flew into my face.

"It's okay!" I called. "It's me! It's Toby."

But then Asher's hand was over her mouth, and any comfort she might have felt from my words was lost. She let out muffled screams and thrashed against me. Then there was more noise, someone else running towards us.

"Here." Asher shoved two of the silver bracelets into my hand, then I felt him grab Callie's arms. "Put them on her."

I wanted to vomit. She screamed, twisting away from him.

"Just do it Toby," Asher yelled. "You have to."

I found her hands and shoved the bracelets over them. She screamed again at the touch of the metal, and I tightened my grip on her. "It's okay," I told her. "We're taking you home."

Asher swore under his breath. "I forgot about the rune line!"

I pulled the piece of chalk from my jeans pocket. "Here."

He took it and crouched down in front of me, scrawling runes across the corridor floor, I assumed.

"You have to get Zo," I told him. Guilt ate at me that I wasn't going after her myself, but Callie was straining against me, swells of Ben's magic wrapping around both of us. I had to get us out, or Ben would strangle us both.

"I'll look after Zo," Asher said. "Just go. The rune line's right in front of you."

Asher gave me a shove and I half dragged, half carried Callie across the line. Nothingness slammed into us from all sides, compounded by the magical rope tightening around us. Then sounds and light rushed in.

I fell forward, letting go of Callie as I did. She sprawled on the black and white tiles of the foyer floor, unconscious, hair covering her face. I landed on my hands and knees, gasping. I couldn't get air into my lungs. I blinked, trying to make sense of what I was seeing. Instead, confusion and horror filled me.

Blonde hair covered her face. The woman I'd just dragged back here wasn't Callie.

Chapter Thirteen

Callie

I hammered on the door. "Elijah!"

Magic flashed inside the room, light flaring out under the door.

"Ben, please! Let him out!" Wind whipped around me, ruffling the pages of the prophecy. Mosby growled low in his throat then started barking his head off. He circled around me, snapping at the wind.

Suddenly he froze. I turned, terrified of what I would see next. A figure raced past at the end of the corridor too quick to see properly. The sound of humming floated towards me.

"Toby?" I yelled. It couldn't be him, but that humming... The prophecy's pages ruffled again as if answering me.

Mosby shot off, chasing after the figure.

"Mosby, wait!" I ran after him. *Toby, wait!* Could he hear me? Was it even really Toby?

I turned a corner, and the humming swelled to a painful, rumbling volume. The figure appeared in front of me. Sparks burst from it. I gasped and stumbled back. That wasn't Toby. I turned and ran.

"Callie!"

That was Zo's voice. I turned back, but the darkness had swallowed her.

"Zo?" I yelled.

She didn't answer. Instead Toby's voice called from somewhere ahead of me. What was happening? Was any of this real?

Elijah screamed. Mosby bolted back towards the staffroom, but I froze.

Which way? Which way?

I couldn't let either of them get hurt.

Callie...

I gasped at the voice in my head. Toby would save us. Toby would get me and Elijah out.

I'm coming, I called back.

I ran towards him. I couldn't see him in the dark, but I heard his voice. His and someone else's, then the muffled sound of Chloe screaming.

"Chloe?" My steps ground to a halt. If Chloe was with Toby, then...

A flash of light lit up the corridor. Toby stood in the centre of it, Chloe imprisoned in his arms.

"Toby, wait!" I ran towards him. The flash burned out, and the humming stopped. "Toby!" I screamed. But they were already gone.

Another flash lit up from the other end of the corridor – Asher and Zo silhouetted in its glow.

"No, wait! What are you doing?" Then they were gone too. The humming intensified once more, crashing down on me. I crumpled under the weight of it. Suddenly there was a figure beside me. I screamed, pushing it away.

"Callie, stop! It's me. It's Joe."

I shrank back against the wall, and slowly sunk down against it to the floor. Joe crouched in front of me, holding my shoulders.

"Callie, what's happened?"

I let him hold me, not caring for a moment about our complicated father-daughter relationship. "Toby took Chloe," I whispered.

Joe grimaced. "Why?"

"I don't know."

Toby didn't know what he'd done. Chloe had stolen energy from Joe. She could steal energy from any of them, and they'd brought her right into the school.

I tried to get up, but Joe held me in place. "You saw them take her?" he asked, his voice low.

What the hell *had* I seen? Toby had taken Chloe, but why?

"Where's Elijah?" Joe asked.

My stomach dropped. "Oh god, Elijah! Ben's got him."

I had left Elijah. I'd chosen Toby over him, and just left him to Ben. I started towards the staffroom, but Joe grabbed my arm again.

"Wait." Joe gestured to my chest. "What's that?"

I looked down, only then realising I was still holding the prophecy. Joe reached out, gently prying it from my hands. It took a moment for me to let go, my hands refusing to unclench. Once free, it fell open on a random page. Joe scanned it, then flicked to the next. I couldn't tell whether he was reading words or more random letters. A range of expressions flickered across his face, and he went very still.

"What is it? What did you read?"

"Nothing." He closed the book and handed it back to me. "We need to hide this. Put it under your shirt," he said.

I did, pressing it to my stomach. Joe's hands started to glow, and a thin vine appeared – half plant, half magic. He wrapped it tightly around my waist, holding the book in place. I let my shirt fall over it.

"That should hold but try not to draw attention to it."

That I could do.

Be silent.

Be still.

Don't let anyone notice you.

Joe took my hand. "Come on. Let's go find that idiot friend of yours."

I stumbled after Joe. The vine he'd wrapped around me felt comfortingly warm, almost like an embrace. "I don't trust you," I told him.

He gave a half-laugh. "That's fair. Your mother didn't either."

"Chloe's stealing energy from you." I didn't mean to tell him that, it just popped out. He slowed his pace, turning to look at me.

"I saw it. She fed it to Ben."

Joe's jaw worked as he chewed that fact over. I couldn't imagine what he was feeling. I might be his family by blood, but Chloe was all he'd had for seventeen years. How could she betray all that? Then again, Ben was *her* blood. Maybe those ties could never be broken, no matter how much you wanted to rip free of them.

Joe started to walk again, slowly. He tugged on my hand, pulling me along with him.

"Why would Toby take Chloe?" he asked.

I shook my head. "I have no idea."

The corridor outside the staffroom was quiet, and the door stood propped open. "E?" I called.

No answer. I glanced at Joe then pushed the door wide. Elijah lay on the floor in the middle of the room. Mosby was curled up beside him, whimpering.

"Oh my god, E!" I ran to his side. He groaned as I touched him. "Please be okay. I'm so sorry I left you. You have to be okay."

"I'll be better if you stop prodding me." Elijah cracked his eyes open. His voice was thick, and blood split his lip. He wiped it off on his hand and sniffed.

I pulled him into a hug. He winced but hugged me back.

"Where's Ben?" Joe peered down the length of the corridor before coming into the room.

Elijah spat a glob of blood onto the floor. "Something happened to him. He started gasping and clutching his chest. I don't know."

"Heart attack?" Joe asked.

Elijah shook his head, then groaned and clutched it. "Nah, something magical, I think. He was covered in sparks for a moment."

Had Toby taking Chloe away done that to Ben? Was that Toby's plan all along? It didn't make sense. The power Ben had wrapped around all of us kept us trapped here; I couldn't understand how Toby had got her out.

"Are you okay?" I helped Elijah up into a sitting position.

He leaned against my knees, using them to support himself. "I've been better, that's for sure."

I glanced at Joe. He paced back and forth, his jaw clenched. I could practically hear him grinding his teeth together.

"Where's Ben now?" I asked Elijah.

"He went stumbling off." Elijah closed his eyes and leaned heavily back against me. "Don't know where, don't care."

I smoothed the hair back from his face. His skin was clammy under my touch, and his cheeks had a sunken look. "How much energy did he take from you?" I asked.

Elijah shook his head, then grimaced again at the movement. "Too much. I hit him a couple of times. He can't punch for shit."

"Can you get up?" Joe asked.

"Yeah, but you got anywhere we need to be?" Elijah asked. "Otherwise, I'd rather stay put."

Joe's eyes flicked between us, and suddenly I was scared.

"I think we're going to need to run," he said.

"Run?" The word cut off in my throat. I doubted Elijah could stand, let alone make a break for it. "What do you think he's going to do?" I asked Joe.

He shook his head. "No idea, but everything's unravelling fast. We have to be ready."

A heavy weight grew in my chest.

"Is Chloe... dead?" Was that why Ben's magic had weakened? "Toby wouldn't have..." I couldn't say it.

Joe shook his head. "No, she's..." He hesitated. "I don't know. I think I would feel it if she was hurt."

If I still thought the Geminus connections were real, maybe I could have believed him.

Without meaning to, my hand moved to my stomach, touching the prophecy hidden there. It felt like Joe had a plan he wasn't letting us in on. I hoped saving us was a part of it, and we wouldn't end up collateral damage.

"You can piggyback me, right Cal?" Elijah patted my knee. "Crap goes down, I'll jump on your back and you run like the wind."

I let out a laugh despite myself. "Let's call that plan B."

"Shh!" Joe slashed the air in front of us with his hand. "He's coming." He moved to Elijah's other side, hauling him to his feet. I scrambled up, putting my arm around Elijah's waist.

"Is this the part where we run?" I asked him. I listened for humming, or some other sign, but no siren-like sound guided our way.

Joe shook his head. "Not yet. Just stay calm, and hopefully we won't have to."

Ben's footsteps echoed in the corridor, slowly coming our way. Then finally, there was humming, but it wasn't the magical kind. It was Ben, a loud, overly jovial song spouting from his lips.

It cut off as he turned into the doorway. He grinned as he saw us, but there was none of the floppy drunkenness from earlier.

"There you all are. Seems my sister's gone a wandering. What do you think team? Feel like a visit home?"

Something inside me seemed to rise up and plummet down at the same time. Home – his home. The school. He was taking us back.

Chapter Fourteen

Toby

I'd like to say that I was calm and rational in that moment. I'd like to say that I took charge and knew exactly what to do about the fact that I'd just kidnapped someone. I mean... of course we had been planning to kidnap someone, but there was a world of difference between grabbing Callie and getting her out of there and grabbing Miss Trager's sister.

A flash of power crackled in the air, followed by an explosion of sparks, and Zo and Asher landed on the stairs, tumbling down the last couple onto the tiled foyer floor. I didn't take my eyes off Chloe.

"No 'are you okay'? No 'welcome back'? Pretty rubbish after..." Zo trailed off as she caught sight of Chloe. "Woah."

"Is that Chloe?" Asher eased himself up and came to stand next to me. "Did we do this?"

I nodded grimly. The three of us stared down at Chloe's crumpled form. Her head was still slumped, her hair falling over her face.

"Is she okay?" Zo crouched down and gently turned Chloe over. A deep welt ran diagonally across her chest, the skin purple and bleeding in places.

"Is that from Ben's magic?" I asked. What had I done?

Asher crouched down next to Zo. He started a healing spell on Chloe. "I think her ribs are broken."

A crackling pop sounded as his magic found the breaks in the bone. The skin on her chest shifted sickeningly, her ribs slithering back into place. I looked away, nauseous.

"This... this is bad, right?" Asher said. "I mean, we really screwed up."

"*You* screwed up," Zo said. "I'd nearly caught up with Callie when you dragged me back here. I would have got her if she hadn't run away from me."

"You were following a dog when I found you." Asher scoffed.

"Following it to Callie!"

"What are you guys doing?" Julianna padded into the room behind us. She stopped when she saw Chloe. "Woah."

"That's what I said!" Zo said at the same time Asher yelled: "It's not what you think!"

Julianna dragged her eyes away from Chloe to stare at him. What Asher meant by that, I have no idea, because of course it was exactly what it looked like.

Julianna opened her mouth, but no words came out. I felt Zo tense, getting ready to hover and Asher rose, taking a step towards Julianna as if he was going to have to rush in to comfort her, but then Julianna started laughing.

"What the actual...?"

Suddenly we were all laughing. I doubled over, gasping for breath as I tried to calm myself. This was not funny... except it *really* was.

Chloe groaned. The four of us all silenced immediately, Asher stepped in front of Julianna, and Zo reached for my arm, squeezing it tight.

"She's waking up!" she hissed.

No shit, Sherlock, I heard in my head, almost as if Elijah had been standing next to me.

Chloe groaned again, and we all took a step back. She slowly raised her head, then gasped and clutched her chest. The welt had faded with Asher's intervention, but I bet it still hurt like hell. Asher flicked his hand, and glowing ropes appeared around her, binding her in place. They weren't attached to anything, but I guess they didn't need to be when they were more of a magical barrier than a physical one.

"What the...?" She jerked her head, tossing the hair out of her eyes. "What is this? Who are you people?"

Well, that stumped me. She'd been chasing us for the last six months. We'd crossed paths so many times as we'd fought each other but apparently, she didn't have a clue who we were. Maybe Miss Trager was right, and they really were completely under her brother's control.

She stared around the foyer, recognition seeming to dawn on her. "Am I... home?"

The word hit something inside me. I'd been expecting her to say something like "back at the school" but of course this had been her home first.

Zo step forward. "We're not going to hurt you." She raised her hands, trying to make herself as nonthreatening as possible.

Chloe's eyes darted towards Zo, but then she looked back at the rest of us. She reminded me of a frightened animal. The reality of what we'd done hit me.

I stepped forward, moving up beside Zo. I raised my hands too, placating. "She's right. We're not trying to hurt you. We didn't even mean to bring you here. We were trying to rescue Callie."

"Callie," she repeated. She blinked, scrunching up her eyes, as if trying to clear her head. She opened them again, suddenly. "My sister... Ursula..."

Zo and I looked at each other. Fear clouded Zo's face, and a similar sinking dread filled my stomach.

Strangely, it was Julianna who took charge. "I'll get her. It's okay, she's here." Julianna turned and started to walk up the stairs. After only a few paces Asher followed her.

"I'll come with you."

Chloe was back to staring around at the room. "It's different."

Because half of it's been blown up several times, I nearly said – blown up, flooded, had plants growing through every orifice...

Chloe stretched out a hand, as if she thought she might be able to reach out and touch the walls with her pinkie. She didn't fight against the bonds. In a weird way, she seemed... content. Maybe we had actually done a good thing, getting her out of there. It didn't change the fact that Callie was still trapped, but maybe it wasn't a complete disaster.

Footsteps thundered above us, and I turned to see Miss Trager racing down the stairs, Asher and Julianna behind her.

"Oh my god." Miss Trager clutched a book in her hands, but she dropped it as she saw her sister. She ran down the last few stairs towards Chloe, stopping just short of touching her.

"Ursula!" Chloe broke into something that was halfway between a laugh and tears. She reached up yet again, as if to hug her sister, but was caught by the rope.

"I'm so sorry. I'm so sorry. I should have trusted you." Miss Trager started to cry too. She didn't approach Chloe though it seemed like she wanted to hug her, just as much.

I didn't have siblings. I had no idea what this would be like, but I could see the bond between them. Even after all these years fighting each other, they still really wanted to be together.

Miss Trager stepped back suddenly, her eyes turning wary. "Are you still under his control?"

Chloe hesitated, then nodded slowly. "Not right this second, but yes, if he comes here then I'll be back under his control."

Miss Trager swallowed, then nodded. "Then we'll have to do everything we can to break it before he gets here."

I glanced at Zo. She'd taken half a step back. I wondered if she was thinking the same thing I was. Perhaps we could just try edging slowly out of the room before Miss Trager noticed us. She was happy to see her sister, but I didn't think that was going to cancel out the fact that we'd completely disobeyed her.

Miss Trager glanced at us and shook her head slightly. "How did this... how did you get her here?"

I cleared my throat. "I kind of just..." I made a motion with my hands as if picking something up. "We used the bracelets."

Miss Trager blinked at me as if that was the last answer she'd expected. "I didn't think that was possible," she said quietly to herself. Something flickered in her face, and I wondered if it was guilt. She almost seemed upset that she hadn't tried just picking up her sister and running before.

"It broke her ribs," I told her. "And I don't know what else."

Miss Trager looked back towards Chloe, anxiety and indecision written across her face.

"We don't have long," Chloe said.

Miss Trager nodded. She stepped towards Chloe, tentatively taking her hand. She shook a little, as if that was a hard thing to do. Perhaps it was. From everything she'd told us, they hadn't exactly been the closest of sisters before this all happened, and they must have years of guilt and anger and grief to work through.

Chloe squeezed her hand. "I'm sorry," she said. "But I have to do this."

Miss Trager's eyes shot up, and so did mine. Zo and I both launched forward, but it was too late. A swell of power rose in the room.

"I have to give it back," Chloe said.

The power exploded, throwing her and Miss Trager back. Both their heads hit the floor hard.

Julianna screamed. Zo and I started forward again, rushing to Miss Trager's side, but neither of us made it. A searing pain ripped its way through me. I stumbled to my hands and knees. Zo landed beside me. Neither of us screamed, but Zo's face pulled back as if she would. I felt mine shape into something similar.

"Jules!" Asher yelled. I turned to see Julianna writhing in similar agony.

Miss Trager lay unconscious, and power shimmered over her. There was so much power coming from Chloe, and we were too close to it.

"Zo..." I tried to say, but no sound came out. She turned to face me. It was like she was slipping away from me, getting smaller and smaller as she disappeared into the distance.

Zo let out a whimper. "Toby?"

I reached for her hand, as everything went dark.

Chapter Fifteen

Callie

I stared up at the school. It grew more imposing with every step, but I didn't care. I wanted to run towards it.

This place had never been a home to me, always a prison, but I would have given anything to be safely back inside it. Instead, I was about to be forced to attack.

Ben took his time, his pace unhurried as he approached his former home.

Elijah brushed the back of his hand against mine. "You okay?" he murmured.

I gave a single nod, not daring to look at him. The prophecy was still strapped to my stomach, and I wrapped my arms over it, reassuring myself.

"Do we have a plan?" he asked.

I shook my head. "Look for threads, I guess?" That hadn't exactly worked out for us so far, but what else did we have?

Ben and Joe reached the stairs just ahead of us. My heart thudded at the thought of walking up them, of opening the door at the top.

Suddenly, Joe gasped. Mosby started yipping, panicked barks calling for our attention. Joe doubled over, clutching at his stomach. Ben stumbled too, his hands flying to his temples. I turned to Elijah, my eyes widening.

"Run?" he mouthed, but Ben was already straightening up.

Ben shook himself and tentatively moved his hands from his face. He'd gone pale, and his eyes flicked back and forth, not settling on anything. "They must have put up a new kind of ward," he said.

Joe was still doubled over, his mouth goldfishing as he tried to suck air in. He leaned heavily against Mosby, the Labrador the only thing keeping him upright.

Ben stepped hesitantly onto the next stair, and then the next. And then he was moving forward again, his pace steady and unhurried. The arrogant confidence of that chilled me.

"Are you okay?" I asked Joe.

Joe nodded, but sweat dripped from his temples and his skin was grey. "Keep walking," he said. He tried to straighten up, but then doubled over again. Mosby licked at Joe's face, anxious to help.

"What's going on?" Elijah asked. "Are you hurt?"

Joe shook his head, but a gasp escaped from his lips even as he did. "Help me stand up," he said, his breathing strained.

Elijah propped Joe's arm around his shoulders. Joe leaned heavily on him and eased himself upright. This was no ward. Joe didn't look like he could stand unaided, let alone walk. Light flickered over his skin, shimmering in a way that made him even paler.

"Elijah..." Joe turned his head, speaking in a low murmur. I caught the word "prophecy" but not much else.

Elijah's face paled and his eyes flicked towards me. I glanced nervously towards Ben. He didn't break his stride, but turned back, frowning as he saw us huddled at the bottom of the stairs.

"Just keep going," Joe said, loud enough for me to hear this time. "Don't let him know anything is wrong."

That I could understand.

Be silent.

Be small.

I slipped my arm around Joe's waist, helping support him, and Mosby squished between our legs, pressing against Joe. We moved forward together. Joe gasped at the movement, and sweat beaded on his forehead, but he didn't cry out. I glanced across him to Elijah, raising my eyebrows. Elijah's skin was still blanched, and his jaw clenched tightly. He stared at me for a long moment, then he slowly started to nod. I frowned. What the hell was that supposed to mean?

Ben unlatched the school door, propping it open for us. We shuffled into the foyer, still holding Joe up.

My breath caught in my throat. Miss Trager, Chloe, Julianna, Zo and Toby all lay on the floor, unconscious. Chloe and Miss Trager's heads were both bleeding. I didn't know what I was expecting, but this wasn't it.

Asher crouched beside Julianna, his eyes wide and panicked. He scrambled to his feet as we entered, moving to stand in front of the group. He spread his hands wide as if he thought he had enough magic to hold us back.

Ben took in the bodies slumped on the ground behind Asher, and something unfamiliar flickered across his face. "What happened? Are they okay?"

Asher shook his head. "What do you care? You did this to them."

"I didn't do this! And of course I care. They're my sisters." Ben strode towards Miss Trager.

Asher sent out a blast of magic. Ben flicked his hand and Asher flew backwards.

"Asher!" Elijah launched forward, leaving me scrambling to hold Joe up.

Asher's head hit the floor. Elijah grabbed him, pulling him upright, but Asher slumped against him.

Asher blinked and his eyes rolled, only barely staying conscious. "You're back," he said to Elijah. Fireflies lit up, marking the broken connection between them.

"Elijah, get away from him!" Ben yelled.

Don't, I wanted to say. Just a moment more and their connection might heal.

But Elijah took a step backwards, almost robotically. Asher slumped down to the floor, holding his head. I reached for Elijah, pulling him close to me and Joe. He didn't look at me, instead staring at Asher. Elijah's breathing was fast, his chest heaving with each inhale.

"Did you just...?" I didn't say it out loud. I *couldn't* say it out loud. A string of fireflies stretched out between him and Asher. I forced myself to look away, not daring to hope.

Ben crouched back down beside Miss Trager. "Hey, little mouse... come on, wake up now."

Miss Trager stirred but didn't wake. Zo, however, opened her eyes, waking. I inhaled, sharply, and Joe squeezed my hand – a warning. I bit my lip, willing myself to stay silent.

Zo was behind Ben, just far enough out of his line of sight that she might be able to ease herself up and get away before he noticed. She slid a hand across the floor, reaching for Toby. He was still unconscious.

Wake up, Toby, I said inside my head. *Wake up, but don't move.* I tried as hard as I could to push the mental picture of what I was seeing to him. If I could just pass it to him, then he could show Zo through their connection.

Ben stroked Miss Trager's hair back from her face, then turned to Chloe. "What did you do, kiddo?" He touched her forehead, and Chloe whimpered. She didn't wake. Energy flowed out of her into him. Too much energy... far too much. This wasn't like with Joe, where she seemed to be voluntarily passing it on. He was taking it from her, killing her.

"Stop!" I yelled.

Ben looked up at my shout. His eyes focused slowly on me, and he frowned. "For a moment, I could have sworn you were your mother."

Anything else I might have said stuck in my throat.

Ben looked around at the foyer, his gaze casual. "Last time I saw this place it was in flames. You remember that, Joe?"

Joe went tense.

Ben's eyes flicked back to me. "Your mother blew herself up right here, Callie. Did you know that?"

Bile turned in my stomach, but I didn't give him the satisfaction of a reaction.

"I figured she stashed her magic first, but now I'm wondering if it all scattered into the walls. It's always been about the school, hasn't it?"

Toby's fingers twitched, and a low hum started in the room. Suddenly, a stream of thoughts flooded into my head – Zo's and Julianna's voices, even Asher's, echoing through the connection now Toby was awake. It was too muffled to make out words. I looked at Elijah. He didn't give any sign that he'd heard it.

"Sammy's magic is gone, Ben." Mr Grandace appeared at the top of the staircase, Miss Caraway behind him. "And it's time for you to let go of everyone else's."

Ben chuckled. "You're all grown up now, aren't you Arthur?"

Mr Grandace straightened, making himself taller as Ben stood and walked up the stairs towards him. Once, I'd seen the headmaster as intimidating, but not now. His stupid cloak was gone, and his devil beard had grown out into a shaggy mess. More than that, he just looked small next to Ben. My captor would crush him if they fought, or rather, Ben would drain the energy out of him.

With sickening clarity, I realised that's exactly what would happen. One by one, Ben would drain us all. His sisters still lay unconscious, perfect targets, and Zo, Toby and Julianna were hardly in a better position. Elijah, Joe and I were all under his control, unable to stop him. This was it. This was how we were all going to die.

Joe shifted, turning his head towards me. "Do you still have it?" he murmured. His eyes flicked to my stomach.

I half raised my hand, wanting to touch the prophecy to reassure myself it was still strapped to me. Instead, I gave the smallest of nods.

He nodded back. "Your mum will tell you what to do."

I frowned. "My mum?"

Joe didn't answer, turning to Elijah instead. "It's the only way to end this."

Elijah nodded.

"Keep him away from her for as long as it takes. Tell the others."

"What are you talking about?" I asked.

Joe turned back to me. He touched my shoulders gently. "I've always been your dad, and I've always loved you."

Guilt rushed through me at his words. I opened my mouth, but he shoved me across the foyer before I could speak.

"Attack!" he yelled.

And Mosby did. The sweet, gentle Labrador launched himself forward, tackling Ben to the ground, and sinking his teeth into Ben's neck.

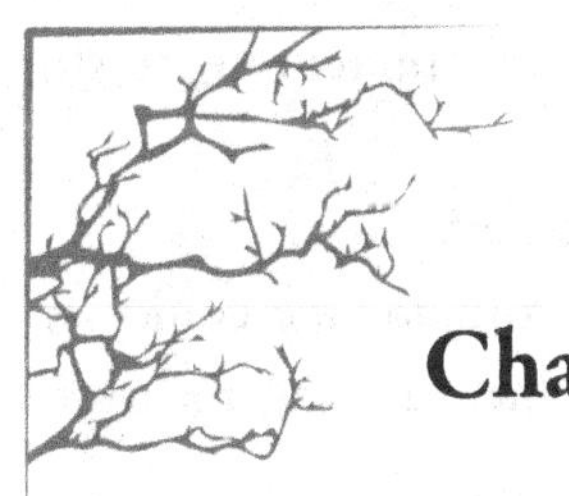

Chapter Sixteen

Callie

"Oh my god!"

Joe launched himself after Mosby, using his body-weight to keep Ben down. I gasped, waiting for the rope around my chest to crush me, but the tightening of the magic never came. Elijah grabbed my hand, dragging me towards Toby.

"What the hell is happening?"

"Just get behind Toby and the others."

I tried to pull away. "No! We'll put them in danger."

Elijah didn't answer, instead picking me up and practically throwing me at Toby.

"Callie!" Toby sat up, sparking into life. He grabbed me, swinging me behind him. I clung to him, my fingers digging into his back in a desperate embrace. My cheek pressed against his chest, and I felt his heart fluttering under his skin. It felt like home.

Elijah spun around, sending out a flare of magic, then suddenly Asher was beside him strengthening it.

"What the hell?"

Elijah put his arm around Asher, clapping him on the shoulder. Asher grinned at him. Their connection. They'd all been silently – frantically – planning while pretending to still be unconscious.

"How did Joe just do that?" I whispered.

An explosion rocked the room before anyone could answer. I stumbled, but Toby grabbed me, keeping me from falling backwards.

The tiled floor of the foyer broke apart, schisms appearing across it. We braced against what remained of the tiles. In the centre of the room, Mr Grandace and Ben fought, swirls of magic crackling in the air above them. Joe and Miss Caraway stood behind Mr Grandace feeding magic into him.

"How is he doing that?" I yelled. Why wasn't Joe under Ben's control anymore? The rope of magic around my chest finally tightened, and I doubled over at the drag of energy as Ben drained me. Elijah groaned, feeling it too. But this time, something felt different.

"No!" I said, and my magic listened. It fought back against Ben's pull. *I* fought back.

"We have to keep Callie safe," Elijah told the others, his voice choked. "Away from Ben's control. She can end this. Joe read it in the prophecy."

Your mother will tell you what to do.

Suddenly, the prophecy was hot against my stomach, burning to be taken out and read. But not here. Not where Ben was close enough to grab it from us.

"Upstairs, the planning room," Asher said. "Mr Grandace put wards around it."

Elijah stooped down, looping his arms under Chloe's shoulders and legs.

"Leave her," Toby said. "She did this to us."

Elijah shook his head. "Joe said to help her." He nodded to Miss Trager. "And her."

"Fine." Asher picked up Miss Trager.

She stirred, waking as he did. "The book…"

"It's okay. I've got it," I told her.

"She gave it back," she murmured, but her eyes were already closing. Blood dribbled down her cheek from the wound on her temple.

"Come on." Toby pulled me to my feet. He, Zo and Julianna surrounded me, rushing me up the stairs. Elijah and Asher followed after us, carrying Miss Trager and Chloe. The stairs shook, knocking me to my knees. I clutched my head. It wasn't just the explosions from Ben, it was the vibrations… that humming. Discordant sounds pressed in around us like we were trapped in the centre of an orchestra tuning their instruments.

Fight back.

I forced myself to stand. Mosby gave a painful yelp, which made me turn back. He ran from Ben, retreating to a corner, tail between his legs.

Toby's arm circled my waist. "Come on, Reactive Girl. Don't stop. You've got this."

At the top of the stairs, he led the way to one of the old classrooms. I paused just inside the door. Pages and pages of red writing lined the walls, all of it swirling, the letters rearranging themselves into new strings of chaos.

"Put Miss Trager and Chloe over here," Zo said. She grabbed a blanket from one of the chairs and laid it out in a corner of the room. She and Julianna helped Asher and Elijah settle Miss Trager and Chloe on it.

The women were both pale, their heads still bleeding, but light shimmered around Miss Trager in the same way it had around Joe. Something had happened. Chloe had done something to them, but whatever it was, it hadn't been for her own benefit. I glanced over at Chloe. She was so still, her face bloodless.

"What happened?" I asked.

Zo shivered, but Julianna stood up taller. She seemed centred somehow, the calmest of all of us in the middle of this chaos. "Chloe arrived back, and like... blasted herself and Miss Trager," she said.

"But why?" Asher asked.

His voice was hoarse, and he seemed to be holding himself back. His eyes were locked on Julianna, like he thought he was going to have to catch her. But she wasn't falling. I could see it in her – a sudden strength and resolve.

"I don't know," Toby said. "Maybe she was trying to weaken us?"

If that was the plan, it didn't seem to have worked. It wasn't just Julianna standing taller. They all were.

"But why did you bring her back here in the first place?" I asked. I felt like I was so close to understanding this, if only the magic would stop flickering around me. There was so much power in the room, all of it trying to draw my attention at once. I couldn't focus on any one thing.

"I didn't mean to. I was trying to grab *you,* but the magic led me to Chloe instead, and—"

An explosion downstairs shook the floor beneath us, sending us all to our knees. Miss Trager gasped, sitting up. She stared straight ahead, her eyes wide but seeing nothing. "She gave it back," she whispered.

And then pain ripped through my chest. I cried out. Toby grabbed me, but I shoved him away, his touch hurting more. I heard a pop as one of my ribs broke. I couldn't fight back against this.

"What the fuck is happening?" Zo screamed.

Bleeding welts opened up on Elijah's shoulder, following the line of the rope of magic. Asher clung to him, pouring healing magic into their connection.

"Enough!" Elijah gasped. "Stop with all this useless shit. Cal, you have to stop this. The prophecy told Joe you can do it. So do it!"

Everyone turned, staring at me. Discordant vibrations sounded as each of their faces turned towards mine, and behind them more and more letters swirled. The pages began to fall from the walls. I clutched my chest, trying to hold my rib cage together.

"I don't know," I said. "There's too many pieces. I don't understand what's going on."

Zo pulled herself up, a fierceness building in her face. "So we lay it out." She picked up one of the sheets of paper from the wall and turned it over. "Ben is stealing magic from us." She wrote that down, with a number one next to it.

Another wave of pain rocked through me, and I whimpered. I couldn't do this. I wasn't strong enough to fight this.

And then Toby's hands were on my face, holding me gently. "It's okay, Reactive Girl," he whispered. "You got this."

I closed my eyes and leaned into him. Slowly, all the other humming notes dropped away, leaving only a soft sound vibrating through the two of us.

"He wants my mother's power back," I said. "His own is unstable. And he said something about side effects of siphoning magic," I said.

"Miss Trager said that too," Zo said. "She was reading a book about it." She and Julianna wrote all of that down.

"Chloe is stealing energy too," I said. "And the magic told you to bring her back here."

Toby shook his head. "I don't know. I think it did? I might have just made a mistake."

"Chloe said she had to give something back," Asher said. "Then she blasted Miss Trager."

Another explosion from downstairs rocked everything. Searing pain rent through my chest, and two more pops. I felt my ribs snap with them.

"I can't," Elijah gasped. He stood slowly, almost robotically.

"Stop him!" I dragged myself up and stumbled towards Elijah. He flung out an arm, shoving me back.

Asher grabbed him, but Elijah threw him off. Power rumbled from Elijah. Chloe lurched upright, barely conscious. If she could have walked, she would have been shambling after him.

"Oh god, Ben's got control of them both." I would be next.

"Calliope..." Ben's voice rang out from downstairs. "Stop fighting me and come join us..."

Pain stabbed through me. Then another pop.

"Let Elijah go," Toby yelled. "Protect Callie."

"No!" I screamed.

But Elijah had already gone, out the door and into Ben's clutches. Chloe stayed where she was for now, but it wouldn't be long until Ben took her. The others crowded around me, pouring healing magic and strength into me. It burned just as much as Ben's power over me, all of it competing and confusing.

"Calliope..." Ben called again. "Come help me find your mother's magic."

Maybe if we just gave it to him, this would be over. Maybe his magic would stabilise, and he could stop this. Let us all go.

I gritted my teeth. He was getting in my head. He would never stop this.

Toby clutched my face again. "Just focus on one thing," he said. "Stay with us."

He brushed my cheeks gently with his thumbs, but I couldn't focus on him. The fireflies around him were too bright. Too much magic that Ben wanted to steal. I stared at Miss Trager instead, at her wide vacant eyes staring back at me from where she sat on the floor.

"The book..." she whispered.

My movements felt slow, but I reached for the prophecy.

Miss Trager shook her head. "The book..."

What did she mean? There were no other books in the room, only sheets and sheets of paper scattered over the floor. There was only one page left on the wall. I stared at it. The red ink swirled, letters rearranging themselves into words.

"She will give back the magic she stole, and they will be powerful enough to stop him," I read aloud.

Miss Trager nodded slowly. Her skin shimmered with the movement. *She gave it back...* Miss Trager hadn't meant the prophecy. Chloe had found a way to reverse the flow of magic. She'd turned it around, pulled it away from Ben, and given Miss Trager and Joe some of their magic back.

Miss Trager shivered, her face pale, but the vacant look dropped from her eyes. Just like Joe she was growing stronger.

"It wasn't just Ben stealing magic, was it? Chloe was always doing it too."

"She didn't know," Miss Trager said. "Don't blame her."

"And today she gave it back."

She'd given Joe and Miss Trager years' worth of power all at once. Somehow that had made Zo, Toby and Julianna collapse and...

"It wasn't just you and Joe she stole from, was it?" I said. "They've been stealing from *all* of us all along."

That's why he got stronger when we used our magic. That's why we could hurt him with force but not power. That's why Joe had trained Mosby to attack.

"It was a spell in a book from the library." Miss Trager rose to her knees, her legs finally steady underneath her. "He burnt it, trying to hide what he'd done, but the magic was too strong."

As if it had heard her, my mother's book lit up. It burned under my shirt until it felt like I would ignite. I ripped it free, throwing it to the ground. Words unravelled from the pages, stretching out to touch all of us. They crawled up my arms like tattoos, then ink began to bleed from them. It burrowed under my skin, until the words were inside me.

They each chose five to siphon from. Two alive, three not yet born.

I could hear my mother's voice in my head, speaking the words of the prophecy aloud.

They shaped the strangers in their minds and siphoned their magic. He wanted to become powerful with their power. But he took too much. He took too much.

"I didn't know," Chloe whispered, her voice cracking with tears. "Ben said it would make me stronger. Strong enough to get away from Dad."

"You siphoned magic from Joe and your sister," I said. "And then Julianna, Zo and Toby. That's why they collapsed too. You started stealing from them before you knew them – before they were even born."

"It was only supposed to be a little. Only what they could spare. They were never supposed to know."

Ben had done the same spell himself. He had taken magic from Mr Grandace and my mother, and then me, Asher and Elijah. But then he had stolen from Chloe too, and all the people she had siphoned from, and it was too much power. He'd taken too much, and it had made him hungry for more.

"Call-i-o-pe…"

The sing-song of Ben's voice made me sick.

"Where did your mother hide her pow-er?"

Ben had stolen so much power already. Why was my mother's so important?

"If he wants your mother's magic so badly, then we have to find it first," Zo said. She put the sheet of paper she'd been writing on aside, turning to me expectantly instead.

They were all turning to me expectantly. "Don't look at me," I wanted to say. She may have been my mother, but my only knowledge of Sammy was through her writing.

Her writing.

The entire room was covered in it – pages of letters copied from her notebook. I knelt down on the floor, picking up the book. The pages were blank. All the words had scattered, crawling off the paper and up over my skin. It was inside me now, words competing with the fireflies and the humming and all the rest of it.

But my mother's power had always been in writing.

I picked up a pen.

Where is Sammy's magic? I wrote.

Drips of ink appeared on my skin like sweat. They ran down my arms, letters forming as they fell. They rearranged themselves on the page, forming handwriting all too familiar to me. My mother's.

I gave it all to you.

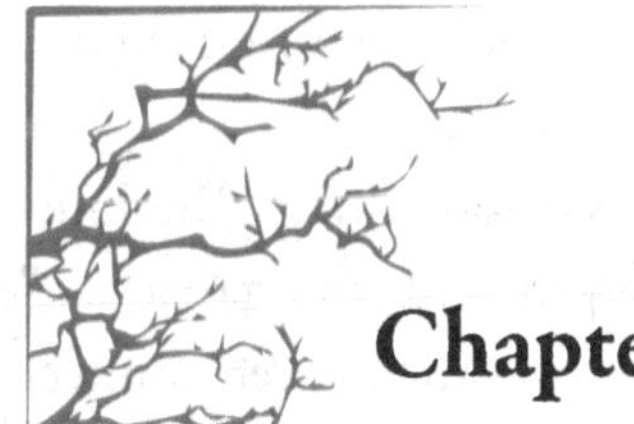

Chapter Seventeen

Toby

The rest of us watched as Callie unravelled... the magic and herself. I closed my eyes, trying to follow everything she'd said. Chloe and Ben had done a spell years ago. Chloe had stolen her sister and Joe's magic, and some from me, Julianna and Zo. It shouldn't have been enough for us to ever notice.

"The prophecy told me to follow the threads," Callie mumbled to herself.

Ben had done the spell too. He had taken from Mr Grandacc, Callie's mother, Callie, Asher and Elijah. But he had also stolen from Chloe, and thereby everyone she had stolen magic from too.

And somehow, that had tied us all together.

"I thought it meant something," I said.

Zo frowned. She seemed to be the only one listening. "What did?"

"The connections between us."

I'd thought the field of power between us had meant something – that my connections to Zo and Callie were special – but they'd all just been part of Ben's sick plan to make himself stronger. We were random strangers who had enough magic for him to steal from, brought together only because Sammy's prophecy told Mr Grandace where to find us.

Zo's face softened. "They do mean something. The links you made protect us. They're probably the only thing that has."

Miss Trager said that too – that it was the broken connection between Elijah and Callie that had made them vulnerable to him. But would any of this have happened if I hadn't linked us in the first place? He'd been dormant for years, hiding out, controlling Chloe and Joe, and stealing so little magic from us we didn't even notice. When I formed those connections, I must have dampened his ability to siphon from us. I'd forced him to come take more.

Callie moved around the room, shifting people as she did. She ran her hand along imaginary lines in the air, as if tracing the connections between them.

I could hear her thoughts, most of them racing too fast for me to catch, but there was one thing that kept repeating. *She will see the threads, and she will follow them. They will all find the way out when they untangle the web.* That's what she was doing. She was untangling the web.

She moved over to Miss Trager, tracing imaginary lines between her and the rest of us.

"But where does this one go?" she murmured to herself.

Through her mind, I saw the lines of the connections light up. There were so many of them overlapping. She traced one back to herself, then on to the prophecy.

"This one is my mother's," she said. "But then where is mine?"

Her magic... was that what I'd been connected to all those months, or had it always been her mother's? Was that why her connection with Elijah had broken? Too many threads of magic trapped inside her, and something had to give?

I reached out, gently touching the thread of magic that ran between the two of us. She started as I did, and a hum almost like a chime rang out in her mind. She took a slow breath, calming herself. This one wasn't like the rest of the competing sounds in her mind. This one sounded right.

"Guys!" Zo said.

I tore my gaze away from Callie. Zo stood by the doorway, her eyes wide. "Chloe's gone."

I spun around. The blanket where Chloe had been lying was empty. It had gone suspiciously quiet downstairs. Callie's eyes went wide.

"She will see the threads, and she will follow them. They will all find the way out when they untangle the web," she said, her words tripping over each other. "They must break the connections, and it must end in fire."

I froze. She'd heard it in my thoughts – that fragment of the prophecy.

Julianna practically screamed in frustration. "That doesn't make any sense! Our connections are the only thing keeping Ben from getting to us."

"Not those connections," Callie said quietly.

I understood now, why everything sounded so discordant in her head. There were the connections I had built, the ones that helped us. And then there were the ones that Ben and Chloe had made. The ones that Sammy and Miss Trager had snapped.

No, I said inside my head. *You can't.*

Miss Trager looked between me and Callie and shook her head. "No. You can't do that. Breaking those connections is too dangerous."

"You did it!" Zo said.

"But it didn't solve anything! Snapping those connections stopped him siphoning from me and Arthur but put everyone else at more risk! He just took more power from all of you when he couldn't get to us anymore. And it killed Sammy!"

"The bracelets." Asher fumbled in his pockets, pulling out the bracelets he'd stolen. He doled them out, handing one to each of us. "They protected you last time. Will it work if we only have one each?"

"It will have to," Zo said.

My eyes flicked around the room. Bracelets already circled Zo, Asher and my wrists, but Callie's were bare. She didn't take one when Asher held it out.

"This is madness!" Miss Trager snatched the bracelet, though whether she planned to force it onto Callie's wrist or ban us all from using them, I wasn't sure. "You can't do this, Callie. I won't let you."

Of course, there was another way. I took a slow step back, heading for the door.

"I have my mother's magic. She gave it to me. She must have wanted me to do this!"

"That doesn't make any sense!"

I slipped out of the room, before I could hear the rest of Miss Trager's argument.

I turned at the landing, stopping before the lower set of stairs which led into the foyer. Ben couldn't see me from here, but I could see everything through the banisters. Chaos surrounded him. Chloe and Elijah lay at his feet, their faces disturbingly pale. Mr Grandace fought Ben partly with magic, partly with fists. Joe and Miss Caraway fed energy to Mr Grandace, but it wasn't enough.

I lit a fire in the palm of my hand. *It must end in fire.* If I burnt my connection to Callie – the one that Ben's spell had created – would the others light up too? Would it burn the ropes Ben had bound them with? I imagined the whole web of threads – mine, and Ben's going up like fuses.

But was I far enough away from Callie that it wouldn't burn her?

I raised my palm. I couldn't see the connections the way Callie could, but I could hear them. I could feel that ping in my stomach when the magic was right.

I moved my hand, waiting for the chiming sound. Nothing. And nothing caught fire.

I swallowed, staring at the flickering light in my hand. Images of Miss Trager's fireball from back when we were first training at the school filled my head. I remembered the pain as the flames had erupted over me.

Toby!

Callie's voice sounded in my head, and then there was a woosh. I stumbled backwards as she enveloped me in something that was a combination of bear hug and tackle. She clapped her hand over mine, extinguishing the flame just as she had done when she leapt across the field to save me from the fireball. She clutched the prophecy in her other hand, and she gestured with it, banging it angrily against my chest.

"Don't you dare!" she hissed, then wrapped her arms around me again. "Don't you dare try do this alone! I'm not losing you like that."

I hugged her back, holding her tight. Her reactive magic had brought her to me. I pulled her tighter against me. The humming turned melodious. Callie's magic really was her mother's, except in those moments when her reactive magic broke through. This was all her. This was what I was connected to. I couldn't break it.

She pulled back to look at me. Pings sounded in my stomach, and suddenly I saw everything through her eyes. Strings of fireflies stretched out around us, all of the threads she had been following.

Two of them seemed brighter than all the others.

Callie gasped. "I've never seen it like that before." Her eyes went wide, seeing everything both through her eyes and mine.

She reached out, touching one of those bright threads. It coiled around, anchoring somewhere deep in her stomach. The other end looped back to the prophecy.

"This is what we have to burn," she said. "This is the connection we have to break."

I reached out, taking hold of the other bright thread. It led down the stairs to the foyer. We peered through the banisters, tracing the magic. It ended at the book Miss Trager had dropped. The spell book – the one from the burnt-out library. The book that had started this all.

Chapter Eighteen

Callie

The spell book lay on the ground at the base of the stairs, its cover bent back. We all peered through the banisters at Ben and the others. They were locked in battle, their focus firmly on each other. Mosby cowered in a corner, alive but terrified.

"What's the plan, Reactive Girl?" Toby asked.

"Yeah, I mean if this is all you got, I'm going to be pissed," Zo added.

All around us, I could see the threads of magic. Everything we did, even if it was to fight Ben, it just gave him more unstable power.

Be silent.

Be small.

"No magic," I said. "Just force."

Surprisingly, it was Julianna who nodded first. "He's weak physically. We just have to get close enough."

"No heroes," Miss Trager said. "We only have to distract him long enough for Callie and Toby to get to the book."

Nods passed back and forth between the group. It almost felt like we should all be putting our hands into the circle to give a cheer like before a sporting match. Instead, we silently walked down to the landing.

"Three..." Asher whispered. "Two... one."

The others all ran down the lower set of stairs and out into the foyer screaming. Ben looked up, startled, but he was too drunk on the power he'd just sapped out of Chloe and Elijah to react. Asher reached him first and tackled him to the ground just as Joe had done earlier.

Toby and I ran for the book. I snatched it up when we reached it and clutched it to my chest with the prophecy. The cover was warm, almost as if it would burst into flame. Ash spread from it onto my hands. This had started in flames, and it was how it needed to end.

We scrambled back up the steps, away from Ben.

"Fire," I said to Toby. "Quickly."

He raised his hands, flames lighting in his palms. My heart squeezed at the thought of setting my mother's book alight, but at the same time, I felt her words shifting under my skin, wrapping me in warmth. She would be here, with or without the physical book.

Toby's eyes flicked back and forth between mine. "Are you sure?" he asked.

I nodded, certain. "This is it. This is how we fix this."

Toby took a long, slow breath. "Then let's do it." He placed his hands on the covers of the books.

A small string of smoke rose up, but the pages didn't catch alight. He frowned. "Why isn't it working?"

The spell book had survived the whole library burning down. We had nothing on that. I stared around at the room. Zo had caused enough fires with her magistations, but I doubted she'd be finding much funny right now. Perhaps we had been right the first time – breaking the connections could cause explosions.

"Perhaps it has to be you, Reactive Girl?" Toby held out the book.

I took it from him, reluctantly. Months ago, I'd sat in Zo's garden, willing flames to sprout from my hands and got nothing but rotting sunflowers. What was to say I'd get anything more useful this time?

"Come on, reactive magic," I whispered.

The pages of the spell book whirled open, just like the prophecy had, but no ink spread off the paper this time. The flipping stopped on a page in the middle of the book.

"Side effects of stolen magic..."

I scanned the list, taking in the information as quickly as possible.

Excessive siphoning may cause magic to become volatile... hunger for power... Mood swings... Weakened bone density... Rapid ageing.

All of this was what we were seeing in Ben, but none of it was helpful.

I skipped down to the bottom of the page where there was a list of warnings.

Never siphon from more than three people from each generation...

Never siphon from reactive magic users...

Well, that explained a lot. No wonder this had gone so wrong for Ben. I froze at the last item on the list.

In the event of death of one of the magic-users you are siphoning from, all power must be absorbed by the siphoner immediately to avoid risk of explosive instability. Avoid allowing posthumous magic to connect with other siphonees.

"Oh my god."

Ben hadn't absorbed my mother's magic, because she'd given it to me. I looked up. I met Elijah's eye across the room. He lay on the floor, so pale and barely moving.

"What is it?" Toby tried to take the book back from me. "Did it tell you something?"

I slammed the book closed. I turned towards him, clutching it and the prophecy to my chest.

"Callie?"

I pulled him towards me, kissing him. He hesitated, then his mouth moved against mine, kissing me back.

I pulled away slightly, leaving my forehead pressed against his. "You know I love you, right?" I whispered.

His eyes widened. *Why are you saying goodbye?* he thought.

I turned, jumping off the top step. A second later I landed across the room, next to Elijah. He sucked in a breath and pulled himself upright.

"Callie!" Toby screamed from the other side of the room. He started to run, but it was too late.

"We gotta try one last time," I told Elijah. The threads of my magic– or rather, Sammy's magic – reached out trying to connect with Elijah's. This was why it had worked with Toby and not him. Because Toby had connected to *my* magic, but Elijah had been coming into contact with my mother's posthumous power – exactly what the book warned against.

Ben's eyes locked on mine. He took a step towards me, but six bodies converged on him pummelling him with fists and kicks. All force, no magic. Even Mosby left the corner, once more growling and gnashing his teeth. Zo grabbed hold of his collar, and then pushed a silver bracelet over his tail. I let out a breath. Good. He needed to be protected too.

I turned back to Elijah. Either he would be able to connect to my magic, and we would be strong enough to shut Ben out, or... he would connect to Sammy's and I would erupt in flames, taking the books with me.

Elijah frowned. Then his eyes flicked to the books in my arms. He shouldn't have been able to read my thoughts, but somehow he always seemed to be able to.

"One more try," he said.

He grabbed my arms and the threads of magic wrapped around us, trying to regrow our connection. At the same time, they forced us apart. Elijah wrapped his arms around my waist, refusing to let go.

"No!" I tried to push him away. "You'll burn. It's just supposed to be me."

Energy built between us, pulsing around the books. Elijah moved his head, bringing his lips close to my ear. "If I had to be stuck with anyone," he whispered, "I'm glad it was you."

"No," I said again. But his arms just locked tighter around me.

There was more I should say. He had kept me safe all these months. He had loved me, even when I couldn't reciprocate. And now we were going to die together, to save our friends.

My hands burst into flame. Searing pain erupted over my skin.

"You have to run," I told Elijah.

He shook his head. "Not until it's done."

I clutched the books, watching the pages ignite. It spread out down Ben's connections. This was it. My mother's power poured out of me, spilling out into the books.

"Stop!" Ben screamed. "What are you doing?"

Flames spewed up as Sammy's magic came into contact with Elijah's.

"It's going to explode. You have to run, E!"

A strange half smile crossed his face. "Joe told me I'd die saving you. I didn't believe him."

I went cold. "What?"

"Get her out of here," Elijah yelled.

I started to turn, but Joe grabbed me before I could stop him. He snatched the burning books and threw me sideways. His and Elijah's eyes met, and then everything erupted into flames.

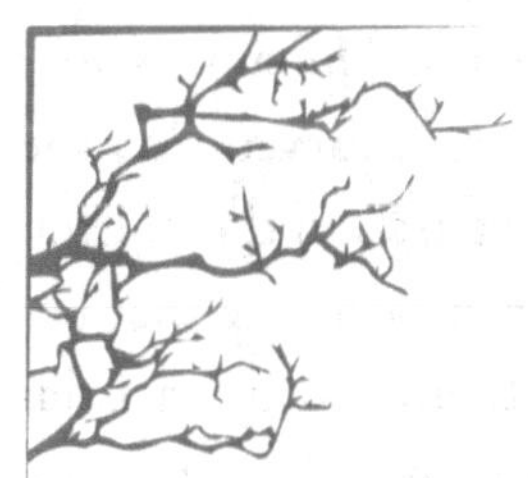

Epilogue

Ursula

My brother didn't die in the fire. He should have perhaps, but I couldn't let it happen. I slipped a silver bracelet onto his wrist during the fight. I hadn't known what was going to happen, but I had figured better safe than sorry.

When he woke, a few days after everything had settled, he had no power. None whatsoever, and he was trapped in the body he had created for himself, excruciatingly old before his time. I set him up in what had once been the sick bay, surrounded by copious plants and flowers. My mother would have been proud, though maybe jealous that my plants never wilted, zapped of energy, in the way hers always had.

I tried to persuade Chloe to stay, but she said she had to leave. She would be back, though, she promised. Once she'd figured out who she was now she was free from Ben's control. I needed to do the same.

Perhaps we all should have left. Continuing in a school where so many people had died was kind of macabre. But the new Principal had insisted. She said creating something new here would be a way to fix everything that had been broken in the magic.

I stood outside the classroom on the first day, watching.

"We should carve our names into the desk," Julianna said.

I smiled, remembering the A.G. and U.T. carved into the desk. I wondered who had added the heart around them. Even now, it made me blush a little. It had never been like that between me and Arthur, but then again, there had never been time. Who knew what life would hold now there was no prophecy marking a cryptic path for us to follow.

"Yeah, sure. Let's be a high school cliché," Zo said.

I smiled. Zo had always been my favourite.

"We should add their names too," Callie said softly.

The others went quiet. Mosby nudged at Callie's hand, as if sensing her sadness. Elijah and Joe had sacrificed themselves to save us, as had Sammy all those years before. Carving their names was the least we could do to remember them.

Toby put his arm around Callie, pulling her into his side. He kissed her forehead gently. If I didn't look at him, I could almost imagine she was Sammy, standing with Joe's arm around her.

"You might have to do it for me, though." Callie held up her hands, still bandaged from the burns.

Toby grimaced. I could tell he desperately wanted to heal her hands for her, but she was determined to do it herself... once she learned how, that was. I admired her for that. And she might actually have a chance at it now Sammy's magic wasn't competing with her own. It would just be a case of her learning to feel safe enough to use her power. So far, she could only do that with Toby, but with time she would find a way to feel safe taking risks – allowing herself to make noise.

Zo pulled out a pen knife. "Come on then. Better do this before the teacher gets here, or we'll all get detention."

I laughed at the thought. I still didn't know what magic school was going to look like this time around, but I couldn't see myself holding any of these kids in detention after what we'd been through together.

"I think we can do better than a knife." Asher closed his eyes and ran his finger over the surface of the desk. His name appeared, carving itself into the wood.

One by one, they added their names followed by the names of the people who had died here. Joe. Sammy. Elijah. At some point, I would ask them if it was okay to add the names of my parents too. But not now. This moment was for them.

I felt a hand on my shoulder, and I jumped.

Miss Caraway smiled. "Sorry, I didn't mean to frighten you."

"It's okay."

"Are you ready for this?" she asked.

I nodded, though could I ever be ready for this? She smiled again, then strode into the room. I trailed after her, enjoying watching her in action.

"All right, children," she said, her voice rich with power.

Everyone scattered, going back to their own desks. They eyed their carved tribute nervously as if they really thought I would punish them for it.

"As you know, my name is Miss Caraway, and I am the new Principal of the school."

I still couldn't believe Arthur had handed over the reins so easily. He'd insisted on taking up a new position – school librarian. Who was I to refuse?

"In the coming months, other instructors will arrive to teach you in the traditional subjects, but for now we are focused on rebuilding your confidence and control with magic, after the ordeal you have been through."

I let out a breath. *After.* It felt amazing to finally be able to say that our "ordeal" as she put it was over.

My gaze wandered over the students. Callie's eyes traced over the names carved into the desk. Sadness flickered behind her eyes, but she also seemed more peaceful than she had ever been. Both her parents and Elijah had sacrificed themselves to save her, and I think she finally understood how much she had always been loved.

Toby shuffled his desk closer to hers. She looked up, and he put his arm around her. I had a feeling those two were going to cause me trouble.

Zo made a face, poking her finger down her throat. Toby rolled his eyes and mouthed the words "deal with it". Zo looked towards Asher and Julianna, the two of them equally full of hormones and puppy love. Zo gave an even bigger eyeroll, but I had a feeling she was finally happy for them. I didn't need magical connections to know what any of them were thinking, most of the time. Nor did they, really.

I would need to start recruiting for more students soon, though. I didn't want to leave Zo as the fifth wheel for too long.

Miss Caraway started to write on the whiteboard, drawing a flow chart explaining the different types of magic. I almost wanted to sit down in the back of the classroom and play student myself. With everything that had happened, my own magical instruction had been haphazard at best.

"You're ready, Reactive Girl," Toby whispered to Callie.

She nodded and glanced at her bandaged hands. "No shit, Sherlock," she whispered back, causing laughter around the room. "Let's learn some magic."

The End

Enjoyed this book? You can make a big difference.

Reviews are the most powerful tool when it comes to getting attention for my books.

As an indie author, it can be hard to get my books into the hands of readers, but honest reviews help me do just that.

If you've enjoyed this book, I would be very grateful if you could spend just a few minutes leaving a review (it can be as short as you like).

Thank you very much!

Also by Helen

Reactive Magic Series

Reactive

Magnetic

Volatile

Explosive

Familiar Magic Series

Familiars and Foes

Accidents and Apparitions (published in Jingle Spells)

Curses and Cousins

Young Adult Books

Broken Silence

Underwater

We All Fall

Children's Books

The Trespassers Club

There's No Such Thing As Humans

Aunt Kelly's Dog

Jenny No-Knickers

Do Fruit Worry About Getting Fat?

Short Stories

Symbolic Death

Find out more at www.helenvfletcher.com

About the Author

Helen Vivienne Fletcher is a children's and young adult author, spoken word poet and award-winning playwright. She has won and been shortlisted for numerous writing competitions including winning the Outstanding New Playwright Award at the Wellington Theatre Awards, making the shortlist for the Storylines Joy Cowley Award, and the finalist list for the Ngaio Marsh Best First Book Award.

Helen has worked in many jobs, doing everything from theatre stage management to phone counselling. She discovered her passion for writing for young people while working as a youth support worker, and now helps children find their own passion for storytelling through her work as a creative writing tutor.

She lives in Wellington with her disability assistance dog, Bindi – a five-year-old, playful Labrador who loves soft toys, cuddles, and can fit three tennis balls in her mouth at once.

Overall, Helen just loves telling stories and is always excited when people want to read or hear them.

Read more at https://www.helenvfletcher.com/.

www.ingramcontent.com/pod-product-compliance
Lightning Source LLC
Chambersburg PA
CBHW011039190726
48290CB00011B/2914